Beak of the Turtle

Thomas Settimi

Beak of the Turtle

ISBN 13: 978-0692210802

Sky Scientific Press
PO Box 7067
Brookings, Oregon 97415

www.skyscientific.com

Also by Thomas Settimi . . .

- CONVERGENCE

Paperback (ISBN-13: 978-1419661518)
Revised eBook Edition June 2012

- ROSWELL 1947

Paperback (ISBN-13: 978-0615829173)
Revised eBook Edition 2013

- THE AVIARY

Paperback (ISBN-13: 978-0692516874)
Revised eBook Edition June 2019

- BEYOND 2020

Paperback (ISBN-13: 978-174544676)
eBook Edition July 2019

Thomas Settimi
tsettimi@gmail.com

CHAPTER ONE

Sichuan Province, China 2565 BC
Five Years after the Arrival

T HE CHILDREN WERE EXHAUSTED, but the travelers dared not stop to rest—not yet, anyway. The village they left an hour earlier was no longer in sight, but they could still hear the intermittent rumbles—less frequent now—that meant the destruction that Hongmin had been warned about was nearly complete. The Visitor who befriended Hongmin told him that he must take his family and leave as the devastation that was coming would spare few, if any, and leave not one stone upon another in the entire village.

They took with them only what the three adults—Hongmin and his wife and sister-in-law—could carry on their backs: provisions for a few days including dried beans and apricots, a few measures of sorghum wheat flour, two prized iron pots, a water bag and several blankets. The blankets would be needed as nightfall in late spring often brought near freezing temperatures to the high foothills of the Bayan Har Mountains. Sheng, the eight-year old

1

son of Hongmin and Li-Hua, carried his favorite toy, a carved wooden ram. Hui-Ying, the couple's three-year old niece, held on to her mother with one hand and clutched a silver amulet in the other. Many years in the future — too many to count — the well-traveled path they followed would become an asphalt highway to Deqen, a city of note in northwestern Yunnan Province and points further south.

THE SUN STILL LINGERED above the distant western peaks when Hongmin led his charges off the trail to a dense stand of Huangshan Pines nearby that would provide refuge for the night. When Li-Hua asked if it was permissible to build a fire, Hongmin unconsciously felt for the dagger hidden in his waistband before acknowledging that a small fire would probably be safe. Hongmin filled his leather water bag from a nearby stream fed by melting mountain snow — a stream that meandered along much of the trail they had followed that day.

Li-Hua dropped two handfuls of beans into the smaller pot with water to boil and then prepared a batter in the second pot, mixing the flour with some water. She smiled when her sister, Jia-Li, unexpectedly brought two dove eggs she had found and stolen from a nest in a low hanging limb nearby. Li-Hua shaped a well in the batter and added the whites and yolk of the creamy white eggs, remixed all with one hand and placed the pot over the coals of the fire to cook.

EXCEPT FOR LITTLE HUI-YING, who had fallen asleep while her aunt was building the fire, the travelers consumed a distinctly bland dinner of boiled beans and mushy undercooked batter bread. Jia-Li set aside a small portion of the bread for her daughter who would be hungry when she awoke. The adults conversed quietly as the fire burned down. The two women expressed concerns about what might be in store for their future. Hongmin told them there was no need to worry. Everything would turn out all right, he promised.

Sheng and the women drifted off to sleep, close together under the blankets to keep warm; together with little Hui-Ying. Hongmin, covered by only a thin blanket, sat with his back against a tree trunk watching as the bright red hot coals of the fire turned first to a dull red and then nearly invisible orange before going out. He listened for any danger, but heard only the night sounds of the forest until he, too, was finally overtaken by sleep.

CHAPTER TWO

Near Washington DC
Present Day

A MANDA MARSHALL was preparing lunch for herself and Roger Atwood in her Arlington, Virginia, condo when the phone rang.

"Hello."

"Hi, Amanda. It's Peter." Peter Gleason was Amanda's literary agent.

"I'm glad you called, Peter. I wanted to ask you about our last statement from the publisher."

"Why? Is there a problem?"

"It's the number of units that were reported as sold. Pretty meager. A big drop from last quarter."

"Well, Amanda, remember that I explained that sales are bound to fall off within a few weeks after the usual publisher promotion period ends. It's pretty normal."

"I was just a little disappointed, I guess. Anyway, what's up? Why did you call?"

"I received an interesting inquiry today. Do you think you and Roger are up for another research project?"

"Sure. Maybe." She paused. "I think so. As long as it has nothing to do with Navy pilots — or Roswell, New Mexico."

Amanda's not-so-serious retort was a reference to the last two investigations that she and Roger had undertaken. Their story of Nathaniel Booth, a Vietnam-era Navy pilot who showed up after 35 years missing in action, was squelched by the National Security Agency. The second, related to the book sales that Amanda asked Peter Gleason about, was their work on the Roswell Incident. Their book presented a rather startling explanation for the 1947 event and Government efforts to cover it up. Despite the thorough research and supporting documentation that the authors provided, critics in the scientific community complained that their explanation of events was simply beyond belief and should not be taken seriously. Amanda's apparent ambivalence about undertaking a new project at this time was completely understandable.

"The woman who called me earlier today was familiar with your work. She —"

Amanda interrupted, "And she's still interested?"

Peter chuckled. "Yes, she is. Her name is Melanie Tsum, but this story is about her father. Years ago the old man translated some engraved symbols from an unusual Chinese artifact discovered in the 1930s. He claimed that the symbols told the story of an ancient extraterrestrial visit to earth, but his work was severely criticized and his reputation discredited by the Chinese government. According to Ms Tsum, the old man turns ninety-eight years old this year. She wants to restore his good name and see that he gets credit for his research before he passes on."

"I can appreciate that."

Roger had been listening intently to Amanda's half of her conversation with Peter Gleason from the adjoining dining room. Now he was leaning against the center island in the kitchen near where Amanda was standing.

Peter continued, "Melanie would like to meet with you and Roger, if you're interested."

Amanda unconsciously raised her eyes toward Roger. "Peter, I need to discuss this with Roger. We'll call you back."

"Just meet her for lunch, Amanda. No obligation."

"We'll get back with you on that." Amanda switched off the phone, picked up the two sandwich plates she had prepared and headed toward the dining room. Roger followed her.

"What did Peter want?"

"He wants us to meet someone for lunch—to discuss a new book project." They sat down next to each other at the table.

"So tell me about it."

"Later. Eat your sandwich."

ROGER AND AMANDA ARRIVED at the Portofino Restaurant in Crystal City a few minutes after one PM. The maître d' escorted the couple to a table in the corner of the main dining room near the painted rust colored fireplace. As soon as they were seated a waiter approached their table with a martini held high in a round serving tray, a young Asian woman following close behind. She wore a white pantsuit with an orange neck scarf and white cotton gloves. The waiter placed the drink on the tablecloth at the open place setting across from Amanda. Roger rose to greet the woman.

"Hi. Are you here representing Ms Tsum?" The woman nodded and smiled.

"I *am* Melanie Tsum."

"I'm sorry." Roger tried not to show surprise at the revelation. "We were expecting someone—"

"Someone older? I'm often told that I look young for my age."

"No kidding," Roger remarked to himself. This woman didn't look a day over thirty—certainly not impossible, but a somewhat unlikely age for a woman with a ninety-eight year-old father. And except for the white gloves, she was dressed in accordance with her youthful appearance.

"You must be Amanda Marshall—" Amanda extended her hand and Melanie grasped it lightly. "—and Professor Atwood. Thanks so much for agreeing to meet with me."

The waiter was now holding the flat bottom of the serving tray against his black server's jacket and asked if he might interrupt the party of three to describe the chef's specialties being offered for lunch. When he had completed reciting the list of available fare, everyone ordered and Amanda proceeded to begin the conversation.

"Our agent gave me a little background when he called, Ms Tsum. We'd like to—"

Melanie Tsum interrupted, "Please, call me Melanie."

"Certainly. As I was about to say, Melanie, your father's story sounds quite compelling. Why don't you tell us more?" Amanda took out a notepad.

"My father has had a remarkable life. When the Japanese invaded Manchuria in 1931, he was studying early Asian languages at the University of Peking. He was conscripted by the Chinese Army and assigned to an intelligence unit, working on breaking Japanese military codes. Near the end of the war, he worked with the OSS."

Roger turned to Amanda. "That was the World War Two predecessor of the CIA." Amanda acknowledged Roger's comment with a nod as Melanie continued.

"He returned to the university after the war as a researcher in the Anthropology Department. One of his colleagues—a Professor Chu from his department—had led an archaeological expedition to the Bayan Har Mountains in 1938." Melanie Tsum paused as their waiter served the individual salad dishes and refilled water glasses.

"Where is that, exactly?" Roger asked. "I'm not familiar with Bayan — what was it?"

"Bayan Har. It's a mountain range in Qinghai Province."

"Qinghai Province? Not helpful," Roger thought to himself.

Melanie could tell from the expression on Roger's face that he needed more information. She quickly added, "That's in southwest China — near the border with Tibet. The indigenous people living there were known as the Dropa. They led Professor Chu's expedition to a large cave that held several graves containing humanoid remains. It was determined that the graves may be four or five thousand years old. The dig they initiated also uncovered a strange disc-shaped object, about eight inches in diameter."

Amanda posed the question, "And you believe the graves and the disc are evidence that we were visited by aliens?"

"Yes, although I much prefer the term 'extraterrestrials'."

Roger had been listening intently and had a question of his own. "I'm not sure I understand. What was it about this disc that led Professor Chu to determine it was alien — I mean, of extraterrestrial origin?"

"It wasn't just one disc. Over the next few days they uncovered several more. Many were quite large, maybe a half-meter in diameter. This group of discs seemed to be largely ornamental, but there were a few smaller ones — the same size as the very first one — that attracted Professor Chu's special attention. Each of these had a spiral groove that ran from a central perforation in the disc out to the edge. Under magnification, Professor Chu found tiny symbols — like hieroglyphs — cut into the bottom of the grooves. There is no known earth technology as old as the discs that could have generated these small symbols."

"So this was the basis for assuming an extraterrestrial origin? Isn't it possible that the grooves and symbols were added much later? As part of a hoax? There are plenty of examples throughout history of discovered artifacts that were later discredited; like the Piltdown fossil and the Kensington Runestone."

"Certainly, Professor Atwood, anything is possible. And in fact, it was later determined that the larger discs were of much more recent origin than the small ones and were probably made by some of the local indigenous people hundreds of years later. Today the discs — both large and small — are known collectively as 'Dropa Stones.' You can find photographs and plenty of stories on the internet touting different theories about the origin of these stone discs. There are also plenty of articles that question their authenticity. But regarding your comment about fake artifacts, you might be interested to learn that the Kensington piece has been the subject of new research which may call into question the prior conclusions regarding its lack of authenticity. I know of one such study currently underway at my school."

"You teach at a college?"

"No, not yet. I'm a doctoral candidate in the Anthropology Program at the University of Virginia at Charlottesville."

Their waiter returned to the table with the lunch entrées. Roger requested another martini for Melanie and a glass of Riesling for himself and Amanda. Melanie continued, "You should know that my father would never knowingly participate in an archaeological hoax, and he had the greatest respect for his colleague, Professor Chu. Consequently, I am confident that the tiny inscriptions on the stone discs were there when they were discovered by Professor Chu's expedition. That dates the inscriptions before 1938 – at the very latest. My father began his decoding work on the discs in 1953 and achieved some limited success after two years. Today it would be possible to etch those small symbols in stone with a precision high-power laser or some nano-technology machine tools, but those technologies weren't invented until much later."

Amanda seemed satisfied with Melanie's argument for the authenticity of the Dropa Stones and the inscriptions; Roger wasn't so sure. There was little further discussion until everyone at the table had finished their meal.

"I UNDERSTAND THAT YOUR FATHER is still living. Is that correct?" asked Roger.

"Yes, it's true. Baba will be ninety-eight years old next month. He is in remarkably good health for now, but — at his age — one never knows how many months or years he may have left." Melanie looked down, pausing for a moment before continuing. "That's why I'm anxious to move forward as quickly as possible. My father's reputation has been all but destroyed by a few Chinese government bureaucrats. They scoff at the idea that extraterrestrials may have visited earth several thousand years ago. I need your help to restore my father's good name."

Amanda posed the question for which both she and Roger needed a satisfactory answer. "What is it that you believe Professor Atwood and I can do to help you?"

"I think — no, I know — that you are able to tell my father's story in a way that will silence his detractors and convince the skeptics that my father is an honorable man who has made a startling discovery of historic significance."

Roger, with his characteristically pessimistic view of most opportunities he encounters, offered an additional concern. "You know that our most recent research concerning the 1947 Roswell Incident has not been well-received by the scientific community."

"Now that's an understatement," Amanda quipped. Melanie smiled at her remark.

"Yes, I've read some of those reviews. But they don't change my opinion of your work. Roswell is a highly controversial subject—one that's been previously studied in depth by dozens of researchers. In contrast, the story of my father's work and the Dropa Stones has never received significant attention from serious researchers, and most of the general public has never heard the word 'Dropa'."

"If we agree to undertake this project, we would need to conduct an extensive interview with your father—maybe several sessions. Do you think we could set up a Skype communication link with him in China?"

"If my father was still in mainland China today, he would be under house arrest, or worse. Fortunately, he was able to leave the country years ago and has been living in Thailand. But even better, you will be able to interview him in person soon. He arrives here from Bangkok in a few days."

"Excellent," replied Amanda, "and what about the Dropa discs? We need to see them—touch them. We don't know at this point if we will have enough material for a book, or maybe just a magazine article. In either case, we'll need to include photos."

"According to my father, there were just five of the special Dropa discs—each identical in size and shape. One was sent to a research institute in the Soviet Union during the 1950s. This was before relations between the two countries cooled off. It has never been returned. The University at Chengdu was in possession of the second, but we believe it was eventually confiscated by the Chinese government. My father was able to carry one of the discs out of the country when he left mainland China. He will be bringing it with him to Washington."

"And what about the remaining two discs?"

"We have no information about them. They disappeared — or were simply misplaced — sometime before Professor Chu joined the faculty at Beijing."

CHAPTER THREE

Sichuan Province, China
2565 BC

IT HAD BEEN TWO DAYS since Hongmin led his family from their farming village on the trek south. The Visitor told Hongmin to *"stay on the footpath that follows the stream until it flows into the wide river."* And up ahead, the travelers could finally see it: the Yalong River that they hoped would eventually lead them to a place of refuge in the South.

The Visitor described a sleepy, peaceful village where Hongmin could provide for his family and where they would be accepted by the local population. They would find it nestled in a green valley, surrounded by mountains and well off the main road. But this final destination was over 300 kilometers from their former home and after three days they had covered less than thirty kilometers.

THE FOOTPATH THAT THE TRAVELERS followed ended at a junction with a well-traveled road running along the eastern edge of the Yalong.

Now they began to encounter many other travelers—mostly couples with one or two small children and some groups of three or four ragtag young men. Strangers all, Hongmin offered and received an occasional nod as they passed each other but there were few smiles exchanged. Almost without exception, the aggregate of the wayfarers on the road in both directions was the very personification of poverty: most were barefoot, with worn and dirty clothing and few earthly possessions.

The Visitor warned Hongmin that their travel would be difficult and potentially hazardous as they might encounter thugs or robbers. And because they would be traveling with two small children, it was unclear what distance could be covered each day. Hongmin knew they had insufficient provisions for a two or three week journey on foot and that the children, especially, would be unable to sustain the pace. As long as they walked at a moderate rate, Sheng was able to keep up with the adults, but Hui-Ying had to be carried most of the time.

Hongmin was told that it would be best if he could negotiate passage with the operator of a river raft or chuán—a primitive sailing vessel. The chuán was the precursor to the Chinese junks that would begin to appear centuries later during the Han Dynasty. Before reaching the river Hongmin had never before seen such a vessel, but now the possibility of completing their journey on the water was fully occupying his mind. Sheng was especially excited to see the boats on the water; he would shout and point whenever another one came into view.

As they continued their journey, the travelers came up upon a watercraft tied up near the shoreline. Hongmin asked his family to wait and rest by the road while he approached the vessel. A middle aged man, considerably older than Hongmin, was seated on a rock near the boat, mending a net. The man looked up when he heard Hongmin approach. Hongmin raised his open hand, waved, and then stopped and asked if he could approach.

The fisherman spoke a slightly different dialect, but Hongmin eventually made himself understood. "Can you take me and my family down river?"

"How far?"

"Maybe fifteen suns walking. It is a place called Chiang-Ri. Do you know that place?"

"Yes, I know of it. But you cannot walk to Chiang-Ri in the time of fifteen suns. Not with your family with little ones. Maybe twenty suns; maybe longer."

"How long is the journey by way of the river?"

"Five suns, if we travel until after dark and start again before light. But how would you pay? You appear to carry little of value."

"Is the cost great?"

"You must understand, my friend. I am a fisherman. I trade some of my fish with the Marsh People so that my family can have rice. I cannot fish while I take you down river, and then I must hire one of the large ships powered by the wind and men who pull on the oars to tow my boat back up river. Many days with no fishing. What do you have for payment?"

"I will show you."

Hongmin returned to where his family was waiting and took his wife aside. He grasped both of her hands in his own and whispered to her. "We must offer your prize, Li-Hua, as payment for the trip." Her eyes fell to the ground and she raised one hand to her chest, pressing her open palm against the piece hidden beneath her blouse as if to protect it. It was a gift and her most prized possession. She began to weep, but dutifully lifted the gold chain from the back of her neck and passed it over her head, raising the amulet from beneath her blouse. She gazed at it longingly for a minute, holding it with both hands. It was similar to the silver amulet that the Visitor had given to her niece. But this one, and one given to her sister, was larger and made of solid gold with an inlay of the finest jade. Without questioning his pronouncement, Li-Hua extended her hands, offering the piece to her husband.

Hongmin returned to the fisherman and his boat and presented the amulet for the man's inspection. He was excited over the prospect of possessing such a valuable piece, but tried hard not to show it. "Is this all you can offer for the safe transport of your entire family to Chiang-Ri?"

But Hongmin was not about to be intimidated by this fisherman. "This piece was a gift to my wife.

Its value is far greater than even your boat and all of your fishing lines and nets. But for it we ask only safe journey and good provisions. I will hold this piece until we arrive, and then it will be yours. You can agree to this trade, or I will offer the same to the next fisherman I see."

"Come," the fisherman gestured for Hongmin's family to board the vessel. "We leave very soon."

THE FISHERMAN GUIDED HIS BOAT and five passengers into the main channel of the Yalong River to begin the journey south. Hongmin sat with his niece on his lap, looking out over the bow and reflecting on the events that led them to this place.

It had been five years since the Visitor's vessel had arrived, crash landing near the village. He and the others at first ran away, fearing for their lives. After all, for three nights preceding the crash a bright light appeared in the sky, rising in the east and passing nearly overhead until it disappeared beyond the western horizon, repeating the pattern every night—five or six times from dusk until dawn. *"It is a sign,"* the village soothsayer told them, *"that a great and evil calamity is about to befall our village."*

The crash merely added credence to the old woman's prediction. There was more to come, she claimed, because the light in the sky continued to appear every night just as before—even after the Visitor's vessel crashed to earth.

On the second day, a few of the villagers— Hongmin among them—returned to the site. As their courage returned, they approached more closely until a few even dared to touch the strange craft — black, metallic, half buried in the earth. There was no sign of life within — not until the following day.

The people of the village could not have known that the crashed vehicle was the third of three scouting vessels sent from the mother ship — the bright light in the sky that appeared to them every evening. Nor did they understand that the vessels were sent from the stars — from a planet much like earth that orbited a star like the sun, but so distant that the light from that star took years to reach the earth.

CHAPTER FOUR

Near Washington DC
Present Day

AFTER THE CONNECTING FLIGHT from Busan to Tokyo, the fourteen hour non-stop flight from Tokyo's Narita Airport was scheduled to arrive just before 3 PM, but it was now 5:30 and there was still no sign of the elderly Professor Tsum. Roger Atwood and Amanda Marshall brought Melanie from her hotel in Alexandria and waited with her at the International Arrivals Building at the Dulles Main Terminal.

Melanie was concerned for her father because the flight information display on the wall nearby indicated that United Flight 804 had arrived "ON-TIME." She considered the possibility that he had missed his connecting flight in Busan or Tokyo. If he was still in Bangkok, she would have heard from him by now.

Amanda explained to Melanie the expected routine for the passengers. First stop would be Immigration. That shouldn't be a problem as Professor Tsum held a Thai passport and would certainly have obtained the necessary visitor visa before he left Bangkok. Then on to U.S. Customs which should be a breeze for the old man if his paperwork was all in order. But it had been nearly an hour since the last stragglers from the Professor's flight picked up their luggage from Carousel #15. Finally, a man in his early thirties and dressed in a sport coat and tie approached.

"Melanie Tsum?"

"Yes?"

"My name is David Bancroft. I'm with the U.S. Attorney's Office. First let me assure you that your father is here; he is safe and in good—"

Melanie interrupted, "Mister Bancroft, are you aware that my father is nearly one hundred years old? What is this all about? He's done nothing wrong."

"We are holding your father temporarily at the request of the Chinese Consulate."

"On what charges?"

"The claim is that Professor Tsum has violated Chinese Antiquities Laws."

"Wait a minute," interjected Roger. "My understanding is that the U.S. has no extradition treaty with China."

"I'm sorry, sir." Bancroft sounded irritated. "This is a matter between my office and Professor Tsum. I'm speaking with Ms Tsum as a matter of courtesy."

"It's alright, Mister. Bancroft. Professor Atwood and Ms Marshall are here at my invitation. There is nothing you can tell me that I wouldn't want them to hear."

"Very well, let me explain. Our courts have taken the position that charging any violation of a foreign country's antiquities laws requires an examination of fact to see if any U.S. Customs regulations may have been breached. There will be a hearing tomorrow morning before a Federal judge to see if Professor Tsum should be charged with the illegal importation of old world antiquities to the United States."

"Should he have legal counsel for this hearing?"

"I asked your father specifically if he wanted an attorney. He told me it was not necessary; that he had done nothing wrong and was confident that the charges would be dropped."

"That's not reassuring. You will be releasing him this evening, correct?"

"Unfortunately, no. But I can take you to see him. I think he'd like that."

CHAPTER FIVE

Alexandria Virginia
Present Day

THE UNITED STATES DISTRICT COURT for the Eastern District of Virginia in Alexandria is located in the Albert V. Bryan Building in Courthouse Square. The court clerk called the hearing participants to order at 10 AM with Senior Judge T.S. Anderson presiding. While the principals in the case and observers to this open hearing looked on, Judge Anderson examined for the first time the summary briefs that were previously submitted by each side. Professor Tsum's brief was exactly that: a single sentence declaring his innocence. The U.S. Government's submission on behalf of the Chinese Consulate was far more detailed and lengthy.

During the short visit with her father the evening before, Melanie Tsum was unsuccessful in her attempt to convince him that he needed legal representation for the hearing. He was adamant; he would represent himself. Meanwhile, the Chinese Consulate had hired a highly regarded District of Columbia firm specializing in international law. An

Asian-American woman would argue their case. Melanie, Roger and Amanda sat directly behind Professor Tsum. Four young Asian men, all rather rough-looking, sat in the last row at the back of the courtroom. After five minutes of reading, the judge set the briefing papers aside, removed his reading glasses and addressed the participants.

"The purpose of this informal hearing is to determine if there is sufficient evidence to charge Professor Tsum with a violation of U.S. customs regulations, pertaining specifically to claims by the Government of China—The Peoples Republic of China—that the Professor may be illegally in possession of certain artifacts officially designated as Cultural Antiquities." The judge looked directly at the Asian attorney. "You are representing the Chinese Consulate?"

"Yes, sir."

"And your name?"

"Diana Li."

"And Professor Tsum—you are representing yourself?"

"Yes, your Excellency." The Professor bowed his head slightly, in deference to the judge. He spoke with a moderate Asian accent, but his English was passable.

"I would think that as a seasoned and well-educated individual you would make wiser decisions on your own behalf, Professor, but this court will respect yours, nonetheless. And you can address me simply as 'your Honor' during these proceedings." Professor Tsum nodded. "Counselor, please proceed."

"Thank you, your Honor. We have reason to believe that when Professor Tsum emigrated from the Peoples Republic of China to Thailand in 1970, he illegally appropriated one or more priceless archaeological pieces discovered during the last century that predate the period of the Iron Age in China. Furthermore—"

The judge interrupted. "Excuse me, Miss Li, but you must know that there is a seven-year statute of limitations that applies to virtually every U.S. Customs law and regulation. Even if you were able prove your charge, there is no agency of my government that could assist in recovery of the artifacts from Professor Tsum—not after all these years. Your argument is a non-starter. What else do you have?"

"Very well, your Honor." Diana Li drew a deep breath before proceeding. "Professor Tsum arrived here in Washington from Bangkok yesterday afternoon. We believe that the Professor currently has in his possession, in either his carry-on luggage or baggage that was checked, one or more of the contraband items."

The judged turned toward Melanie's father. "Is that true, Professor?

"No, not true."

"I think we can clear this matter up quickly. Counselor, do you have a copy of the Professor's Customs Declaration?"

"Yes." Diana Li removed the document—the Form 6059B—from a manila folder and handed it to the court bailiff who presented it to Judge Anderson. It took only a moment for the judge to examine the document.

"According to this, you had nothing to declare. Is that correct, Professor?"

"Yes, your Honor."

"And were you required to open your bags for an inspection?"

"No. I—"

"Excuse me, your Honor." Diana Li interrupted, "Unless the customs agent has reason to believe the declaration may be fraudulent, passenger baggage is routinely passed without undergoing inspection."

"We're aware of that, counselor." The judge turned toward the bailiff. "Henry, were Professor Tsum's bags brought here this morning from the Dulles Immigration Detention Center?"

"Yes, sir. They're in the jury deliberation room."

Judge Anderson cleared his throat, then looked first at the Professor, then Diana Li before speaking. "I'm loathe to proceed in this manner, but let us resolve this issue this morning. Professor, would you permit an inspection of the contents of your baggage in this courtroom, in front of everyone here present?" The Professor answered in the affirmative. "And Counselor Li, are you willing to accept—without appeal—any ruling I make this morning after a careful consideration of the outcome of the inspection?" Diana Li turned her head to look at the men in the back row. The one near the aisle nodded and Diana turned back to reply to the judge.

"Yes, your Honor. After an impartial examination, we agree not to appeal any ruling you make today."

"Bailiff . . . ." Without waiting for the request, the bailiff left the courtroom through a side door and then returned moments later carrying a medium-sized, old-style Samsonite suitcase and a fabric carry-on bag. The bailiff placed the bags on the table in front of Professor Tsum, then stood at attention, facing the judge, with his hands together behind his back. "Proceed, Henry. Remove all the articles from the bags and place them on the table. Counselor, please step to the table so that you can observe more closely."

The bags were opened and the bailiff proceeded as he was directed. It took less than five minutes to remove everything from the two bags: a brown suit, several shirts and ties, suspenders, some undergarments and an extra pair of shoes.

The judge observed patiently with his hands resting upon one another on the desktop surface in front of him. From the carry-on, the bailiff removed a small toiletries bag containing the usual razor kit, hair brush and comb and dental care items. At the bottom of the bag were some notebooks and a ringed binder as well as some hardbound books — two in English and what appeared to be a technical book printed in Traditional Chinese.

The judge waited for Diana Li to look over all of the Professor's belongings and examine the empty bags. "Anything that could be classified as an antiquity, counselor?"

"No, sir."

"Then this hearing is over." Judge Anderson banged his gavel. "Professor, you are free to go." At the back of the courtroom, the man seated near the aisle jumped to his feet, yelled something in Mandarin at the judge, and stormed out of the courtroom. His three associates quietly rose and followed him. Melanie left her seat and joined her father who was stuffing his personal effects back into his bags.

Amanda whispered to Roger, "What was all that about?"

"Apparently, someone is unhappy with the judge's decision."

Professor Tsum held his daughter close and whispered to her in a Sichuan dialect, "You should have believed me when I told you there was nothing to worry about—that I would be cleared of any wrongdoing."

"You could have told me last evening that you decided not to carry the object with you."

"It was better that you did not know until now. But not to worry—it is safe and on its way here—FedEx."

ROGER DROVE TO THE STARBUCKS nearby on Ballenger Avenue for some hot tea for Amanda,

Melanie and the Professor and coffee for himself. After the patrons at a neighboring table left the coffee shop and there were no other strangers within earshot, Melanie brought up the subject of the Dropa disc as she knew that Roger and Amanda would be wondering about it. This time she spoke in English.

"How is it, Father, that you decided not to carry the disc with you on the airplane?" The old man hesitated, and noting his reluctance to speak, Melanie quickly added, "It's OK, Father. My friends are here to help us. You need to tell them everything and not hold anything back. With our help, they will tell the truth about your discovery and silence all who dared to criticize you."

The Professor nodded and then spoke. "I was ready to carry it with me, but two days before departure I had very bad feeling. I leave China many years ago, but I think that maybe they not forget about me. So I have the Dropa Stone shipped to my friend. He owns engineering company in Washington area."

"Good decision, Professor."

ROGER AND AMANDA LEFT THEIR VISITORS at the lobby entrance to the hotel after the four agreed to meet together in Melanie's suite the following day. But on the way back to the condo, Amanda's cell phone rang, and she retrieved it from her purse.

"Hello, Amanda?" The tone of the caller's voice was unmistakably alarming.

"Yes. What is it, Melanie?"

"Someone's been in our suite. Everything is turned upside down."

"Are you and your father all right?" asked Amanda.

"Yes, we're OK. We didn't walk in on anyone, thankfully."

"Roger and I are coming back to the hotel. We'll be there in a few minutes."

CHAPTER SIX

An Earth-Analog Planet in
the Ross 614 System, 2585 BC

THE DEBATE HAD GONE ON FOR YEARS, both in the halls of government and among the citizenry. The Patricians argued that funding for the Grand Expedition must be approved for the sake of scientific advancement, despite the tremendous cost. The other side — the Subordinates — called it folly. They held the conviction that the Treasury surplus made possible by several consecutive years of a highly prosperous economy should instead be used solely to improve the lives of all the less fortunate citizens of their world. The third largest political party and voting bloc, the Disciples and the Believers that supported them, held no official position on the matter — not at first, anyway.

The Unification Government had been in existence for 67 years. It unified for the first time the seventy-eight formerly independent Enclaves making up the planet. Unification occurred after fifteen years of inter-Enclave wars that killed half the population of the planet and left most of the other half destitute.

The coalition of Enclaves that represented the "winners" in the war became the pattern for the new government. The new Constitution established three branches of government. The Law Makers represented the only branch directly elected by the citizenry. Each Enclave elects from one to five Law Makers, the number determined by a census conducted every eight years. This legislative body has a total of 256 members, elected every four years for a four year term. From and by this body, three Administrators are chosen; one every two years for a six-year term. The Unification High Court consists of seven judges, selected by unanimous vote of the Administrators with confirmation by the Law Makers. High Court judges serve for life.

It became clear almost from the beginning that none of the major political parties enjoyed majority support from the citizenry, and so a coalition of various factions was needed in order to implement nearly every major government initiative.

The Grand Expedition had been proposed several years earlier; made possible by two extraordinary achievements by the scientific community. The first of these was the discovery of a planet in a nearby star system, nearly fourteen light years distant that might be able to sustain life. It orbited about a star along with seven other major planetary bodies and a belt of asteroids—perhaps the remnants of another planet broken apart by tidal forces or gravitational effects from its planetary neighbors.

The energy intensity of the star and distance to it made for a level of insolation at the surface of the planet to be similar to their own. The planet had a single large natural satellite. The discovery of this planet was made by their largest space-based telescope.

The second achievement was development of the Impulse Magneto-Plasma (IMP) propulsion system. A spacecraft configured with the latest IMP Drive is able to slowly accelerate, eventually attaining a maximum speed equal to 99% of the velocity of light. At this speed, nearly thirty years would pass while the spacecraft made a roundtrip journey to the distant planet. But for the travelers *aboard* the spacecraft, only about four years will have passed. This phenomenon is the result of time dilation, a relativistic effect that becomes significant at near light speed.

BUT AFTER MORE THAN FIVE YEARS of debate the citizenry grew tired of the controversy and it appeared that the idea of the Grand Expedition would be shelved, perhaps until some future time when a more enlightened generation might advance the project anew. But as is often the case, an unpredictable event can sometimes change the course of history. And so it came to pass that a prominent scientist underwent a spiritual conversion and joined the leadership of the

Disciples Party. He argued that the Grand Expedition should go forward, if for no other reason than it might finally provide the answer to the fundamental question about life on their planet. That is, where and how did intelligent life originate?

As his influence grew in the Party, the scientist-turned-politician was able to convince many Disciple Party lawmakers to join with the Patricians in support of the Grand Expedition legislation. The coalition was forged and the bill was passed and sent to the Administrators for approval.

But the opposition was not ready to give up. If the bill had passed with a two-thirds majority of legislators, only two of the three Administrators would be needed to approve it. But with just a simple majority of legislators, the Constitution required a unanimous vote of all three Administrators for it to become law. The holdout Administrator came from the ranks of the Subordinates and was prepared to cast a negative vote, effectively killing the bill. Only after approval of a rider to the bill, increasing spending on social programs by eight percent globally, did the third Administrator agree to lend his support to the Grand Expedition.

One of the key provisions of the legislation permitted the expedition party to spend up to five years on the destination planet if the Commander-in-Charge deemed it necessary to assure the final success of the mission.

Once it became clear that the Grand Expedition was no longer simply a topic for debate, but was a real project that would be supported and funded by the Unification Government through to completion, a sense of excitement spread throughout every Enclave of the planet. For the Patricians and their citizen supporters, the victory after the long-fought battle was sweet. Even the Subordinates — with their list of underfunded programs that would soon benefit from a new influx of resources — began to see that the economic activity resulting from such an ambitious project could not help but benefit their constituents as well.

But the greatest impact was seen in the life and times of the Disciples and their citizen followers, the Believers. A spiritual revival was sweeping across nearly every Enclave of the planet. Citizens everywhere could be seen and heard, reciting passages from the ancient Sacred Scrolls — about the Creator and how he fashioned their planet in only seven days, filled it first with plants and animals and then breathed life into the first citizen couple "whose progeny would eventually outnumber the stars in the heavens."

Despite the best efforts of the engineers and scientists supporting the early research and development work for the project, it was estimated that the overall probability that a space craft could reach the new planet and return home safely was barely sixty percent and that the chance of a catastrophic failure at nearly forty percent was unacceptably high. The greatest risk, it seems, was not in traversing the huge distance to the destination planet, but rather the transit to and from the planetary surface using the auxiliary excursion vehicle to be carried aboard the mother ship and dispatched after orbit around the destination planet was achieved. After several weeks of study, it was proposed that three smaller scouting vessels be included in the mission instead of the single larger excursion vehicle. With this mission change engineers were able to predict with 95% confidence that at least one of the three scouting ships could successfully land upon and explore the surface — cataloging flora and fauna — and return safely to the mother ship.

Exactly four years to the day after the Administrators approved the Grand Expedition, the IMP-powered Star Ship was ferried up into low orbit in preparation for the beginning of the greatest adventure in the history of the Unification. Among the Believers there was little doubt that the mission participants would return with incontrovertible scientific evidence that would corroborate the authenticity of the Sacred Scrolls and the existence of the Creator.

CHAPTER SEVEN

Alexandria Virginia
Present Day

WHEN ROGER AND AMANDA arrived at Melanie's suite, the hotel manager was still offering apologies to Melanie and her father. A new suite was being prepared and a bellman stood by waiting while Melanie gathered personal belongings that had been strewn about in one of the two bedrooms. The mattresses had been tossed and the cushions from the chairs and sofa were scattered about the rooms. But as near as she could determine, nothing was missing. Melanie thanked the manager for his concern as he excused himself and left the suite.

"Who would have done this?" Amanda posed the question to no one in particular.

"My bet would be on those four fellows in the back of the courtroom this morning — the ones who seemed displeased with the judge's decision," offered Roger.

Melanie responded, "Maybe not those four, but maybe some of their friends. The manager reviewed the entry logs for this suite. He told me that the maids had come and gone by 9:30 but there was another entry recorded at 10:35."

"That's just after the Judge made his ruling and those guys left the courtroom."

"Can I help you get your things together, Melanie?" Amanda offered.

"I think I have everything, but thank you."

Amanda continued, "Do you think the Chinese Consulate would hire some thugs to break into your room and do this?"

Roger interrupted. "Technically, no one broke in. Someone let them in or they had a properly coded entry key card for the lock."

"Thank you for that, Roger. But the point of my question was whether or not the Chinese government was behind this."

Melanie sat at the edge of her bed and looked up at her father. "I thought after all these years they would finally leave our family alone. I was wrong. My government has long had people and organizations lurking in the shadows to do their bidding in this country. There are several Asian gangs operating in this area. Any one of them could be responsible."

ROGER AND AMANDA RETURNED to the hotel the next day at quarter past one. A hotel steward was waiting to serve lunch for four in the main room of Melanie's new suite. Embarrassed by the events of the previous day, management had moved

Melanie and her father into the hotel's Large Executive Suite. The new accommodations were three times more spacious than the former and included more amenities, including a fireplace and a well-stocked bar.

"We're so sorry for being late." Amanda was profusely apologetic. Roger didn't think it was a big deal; they were only fifteen minutes late.

"No problem," offered Melanie. "But come and sit. I've ordered a light lunch for us." Amanda noted that her host again wore the white cotton gloves as she had in their previous meetings—distinctly inconsistent with the rest of today's casual ensemble of jeans, short sleeve blouse and canvas shoes. *"Maybe she has a skin condition,"* Amanda thought to herself.

Once seated, Roger requested a fork and knife. Everyone else was adept at using chop sticks. He tried not to show the sense of mild disappointment he felt after the meatless plates of vegetables and noodles had been served. But after his first taste he voiced a favorable opinion, "This is really delicious."

When lunch was over, the party of four relocated to an alcove area at one end of the suite. Two overstuffed chairs and a sofa were arranged about a heavy marble-top coffee table. Once they were seated, Melanie expressed a concern to her guests—a concern that she knew her father was feeling as well. "I'm not sure how you want to proceed with this."

Amanda was quick to reply. "This story is all about Professor Tsum. I believe he can best tell it for himself." The Professor nodded in appreciation of Amanda's expressed opinion.

"If you have question at any time, not to hesitate to interrupt me. Just ask." While the suite steward poured fresh cups of hot tea, Amanda removed a small voice recorder from her purse, switched it on and placed it on the marble table top. Professor Tsum began to tell his story.

"I WAS STUDYING AT UNIVERSITY in Peking when Japan started war with my country. It was a hard time for the Chinese people. Many millions were killed by the enemy before the war was over. But it was also the first time in many years that the country was united. We set aside political differences in order to defeat the invader. So the Communist Party of China and the Kuomintang opposition stopped fighting against each other and joined together to end the enemy occupation.

"But when the war was over, fighting between political factions resumed. I return to the University. The staff at school try not to show support for one side or the other. All we want is to be left in peace to teach and do our research. In 1949 the Communists — I guess you call them Red Chinese — under Chairman Mao Zedong declared victory and new government was formed. The remaining Kuomintang army and supporters escaped from the mainland to Taiwan."

"Is that where you first met Professor Chu, at Peking University?"

"Yes. It was a few years later, in 1953. By then, my school had become known in China as the University of Beijing, although the old name continued to be used in the West for many years. Professor Chu was new to Anthropology Department, and they invite him to give lecture to staff and interested students. He gave long talk about his expedition from fifteen years earlier. It was well organized expedition; very serious research.

"Many in China knew of legend from ancient times, about travelers who came from the stars and taught the Dropa people much about agriculture and making tools of iron. So the purpose of expedition was to discover if legend was true. Six men make trip to Bayan Har with Professor Chu."

"Was the expedition sponsored by the University, or maybe the Chinese government?"

"In 1938 Professor Chu was a researcher at Chengdu University, but no funding came from the school or the government. I learn much later that before Communist takeover that Professor's family had large land holdings in China and that Professor Chu paid for entire expense of expedition.

"After the Communists take power they institute land reform and nearly all large private land holdings were taken over by the government. Many land owners were killed. No one know what happen to Professor Chu's family, but the Professor himself was always under surveillance by government agents after he arrive in Beijing."

Amanda wanted Professor Tsum to tell more about the 1938 expedition. "Can you tell us more about the expedition itself?"

"Certainly. Professor Chu told me that trip was planned for middle of summer so that weather in the mountains would be favorable. They arrive and set up camp on last day of July near Dropa village. The village people speak with strange dialect—difficult for members of the expedition to understand. But finally they make friends with villagers.

"After a few days, the village chief tell Professor Chu about special cave that is half-day walk from village. They travel there next morning and find opening carved in solid stone wall on side of mountain. Very unusual. Cave is maybe two meters high and one meter wide; six or seven meters straight into mountain. It is very hard rock. Maybe granite. At end of seven meters, the cave opens to a round room seven or eight meters across.

"With light from lanterns the travelers can see places on the wall that are black with soot—burned from torches that were maybe used for some ceremony. There is also art work on walls, but Professor Chu think that drawings were added much later. Could be less than three thousand years old, but cave itself was probably much older."

"How was the dating of the art and the cave itself determined?" Roger asked.

"Art work similar to other cave drawings found in province was previously dated with accuracy using radiocarbon analysis of charcoal pigment. But more important: In floor of round room there were several depressions found — graves with humanoid skeleton parts inside. Many parts were missing, but carbon dating showed that bones were older — at least four thousand and maybe up to six thousand years old."

"You said these were humanoid remains? Not *human* remains?"

"Humanoid — yes. But there is no DNA in such old bones that can prove they are human. There is much doubt also, because of all the bones of hands and feet that could be found intact or reassembled, they have each four phalanges, not five."

Professor Tsum's last statement grabbed Amanda's immediate interest and attention. "You're telling us, Professor, that the skeletal remains found in that cave were from humanoids that had only four fingers and toes on each hand and foot?"

"That is correct, Miss Marshall."

Roger looked directly at Professor Tsum and asked, "Do you have any independent proof of this claim? Were any of the skeletal remains sent back to the University and reassembled?"

"No. I can only report to you the information that I read in a paper that Professor Chu published at Chengdu University. The paper documented observation on site by members of the original expedition. According to Professor Chu, the Dropa chief eagerly traded the cache of discs for a pocket watch and ring and some canned goods but would not permit removal of any bones from the cave. I read this paper at University library, but there is no longer a record of this document."

Roger and Amanda gave each other a quick suspicious glance. *"How convenient,"* thought Roger, *"that no supporting evidence for Professor Chu's claims seems to be available."*

"Professor Chu also reported that other artifacts were found outside the cave, near the village. His team find crudely fashioned plows, shovel parts and knife blades. It was determined that they were very old, but could not be dated."

"Parts such as these," remarked Roger, "could be of recent origin—maybe less than one hundred years old."

"That is true, Professor Atwood, but a metallurgical analysis determined that many of these old parts were made from high strength titanium alloy—an unlikely find from even the present day in this remote part of country." Professor Tsum did not fail to see the expressions of doubt on the faces of the two Americans. "Professor Atwood—Miss Marshall—I do not know how to convince you of my sincerity."

Amanda explained, "Your sincerity is not an issue. Please understand, Professor Tsum. If you were part of the 1938 expedition, we could easily believe your direct testimony, but you are asking us to believe events that were only told to you—or that you read — and findings that you did not determine for yourself."

Melanie started to take exception to Amanda's statement, but Professor Tsum quickly cut her off. "Let me answer, Daughter. I understand Miss Marshall's concern. A good journalist or investigator is trained to be skeptical — to demand proof. I wish that Professor Chu was alive today and here to speak for himself. But for first part of this story — for events that occur before I even meet Professor Chu, I must ask that you accept for now and to please reserve final judgment until I can explain what I learn about the Dropa Stones."

"I think we can do that," offered Amanda.

CHAPTER EIGHT

Sichuan Province, China
2565 BC

JUST FIVE DAYS after embarking on the trip south, the fisherman guided his chuán to shore, grounding the vessel on the sandy beach at a turn in the river. Hongmin's family was happy to disembark and finally stand on solid ground once again.

When Hongmin asked for directions to their final destination, the fisherman replied, "I have never traveled to Chiang-Ri, but others have told me it is beyond the mountains to the east." The fisherman pointed to a cloud-shrouded peak, inland from where they stood on the bank of the river. "If you walk until sunset today, you can reach the entrance to the Valley of Chiang-Ri before the sun sets tomorrow."

Hongmin presented his wife's gold and jade amulet to the fisherman, as had been agreed upon before the river trip south. He bowed to the fisherman and spoke with conviction, "Thank you for providing safe passage for my family." As the travelers made their way from the beach in the direction east, the two children stopped for a moment, turned and waved at the fisherman. He acknowledged the gesture with a return wave.

It was less than a hundred meters along the footpath from the riverbank to the main road—the road running along the length of the river. As Hongmin and his family crossed that road, he wondered to himself if they would ever have reached this point traveling the entire distance on foot. Probably not, he thought. Hongmin bent his body forward and raised his niece upon his back, encouraging her to hold on with her arms about his neck. He then set off along the trail leading up the side of the mountain with the rest of the family following close behind.

The trail presented few hazards, but was nonetheless difficult due to the steady upward grade. After the first hour, the women were clearly tiring. Li-Hua pleaded with her husband, "Please, Hongmin, we must stop and rest for a while."

Hongmin chided her, "Woman, you have become soft during the time we were carried on the water. Think only of putting one foot in front of the other, and ignore the ache in your limbs. We will rest in due time." Hongmin urged them forward, but before the second hour had passed, he again stopped and turned, and seeing that the rest of the family had fallen behind, he lowered Hui-Ying from his back and waited for the others to catch up. Even Hongmin had become weary.

THEY RESTED FOR NEARLY AN HOUR. When her strength had returned, Li-Hua opened her backpack and brought out some of the dried fish and cooked rice that the fisherman had given her and served a meal to the family. After he had eaten, Hongmin closed his eyes for a few minutes, but he dared not fall asleep. He knew that the family would follow his lead and it was important that they travel a greater distance today so that they can reach their final destination before nightfall tomorrow.

Now it was time for them to move on and Hongmin motioned for Hui-Ying to come closer so that he could lift her upon his back. But instead she ran ahead up the trail. "Hui-Ying is big girl and there is no need to carry her. She can walk," the little girl called out to her uncle, referring to herself in the third person.

It was still daylight when Hongmin convinced himself that the family had traveled far enough up the mountain for one day and they could stop for the evening. Hui-Ying had fallen asleep on her uncle's back, having asked to be carried again only minutes after defiantly declaring her intention to walk up the mountain on her own.

The family had encountered no other travelers along the trail—neither moving up nor down the mountain. Hongmin decided that they needn't fear for their safety on this trail and so he began to gather twigs and dry branches to build a fire. The fire would be welcome for the air at this altitude was already crisp and the expectation was that the evening would be much cooler.

While Jia-Li helped her sister with the evening meal, the children played close by, hiding from each other behind the bushes and large rocks. The women would often look up from their work to make sure the children had not wandered off. But before the meal was served, young Sheng ran to where his father sat near the fire and cried out, "Papa, there is something coming down the trail. I heard a noise. Do you think it is a bear?"

Hongmin stood up quickly and pulled the dagger from his waistband. "Get your cousin and bring her near the fire — quickly," he said. Hongmin ran up the trail, past where the children had been playing and called out, "Who is there, coming toward my camp?"

A male voice called out to him, "It is just my wife and I, peasant travelers. We journey to the river. We have no weapons and mean you no harm. We ask that you let us pass in peace."

"Come close to the fire so that I can see you." As the couple approached, Hongmin returned the dagger to his waistband. They were young — and thin. Almost emaciated. They carried no supplies and appeared to have no possessions except for the threadbare clothes on their backs. The young woman looked very tired and Li-Hua asked her to come close to the fire and rest.

"You must be hungry. We have some fish and rice." Li-Hua served the young couple first, then her husband and sister and finally the children. She saved only a few bites of rice for herself; there was no more fish.

The couple ate ravenously, but before he was half-finished, the young man stopped suddenly and spoke. "My wife and I are very grateful. It has been three days since we left the river, and except for some grubs and roots, it was the last time that we ate."

Hongmin was puzzled. "I don't understand," he continued, "You were at the river three days ago?"

"Yes."

"And you came up the mountain with no provisions, and now you wish to go back to the river?"

"Yes. We had been living in the South—in an empty house we found near the river nearly one year ago. I catch fish from the river and my wife grows some vegetables. But maybe seven suns ago, a man comes into the house at night and he beats us. He says that he is the owner of the house and we must leave. We have no home and no food, but a stranger on the road near the river tells us that we should go to Chiang-Ri—that there the land is fertile for growing crops and the people are friendly. I could find work until we can build a house and grow our own food."

"It sounds as if you were given good advice," Hongmin remarked. The two older women—Li-

Hua and Jia-Li — were listening with rapt attention as the young man spoke. "So why are you now going back down to the river?"

"Have you been to Chiang-Ri?"

"No," replied Hongmin.

"It took the time of two suns walking to reach the mountain pass that is the entrance to the Valley of Chiang-Ri. But before reaching the pass, one must cross the footbridge over a deep gorge. There is no other entrance to the valley. The bridge is made of rope and carved planks and is maybe one hundred paces long across the gorge. But the bridgehead is guarded by strong men with swords and bows with deadly arrows. They ask to see my wife's open hands, and she shows them. Then one of the guards asks the name of the person that told us to come to Chiang-Ri, but I never knew the name of that stranger. And so they turn us away. My wife cries but we are told to go back down the mountain. We are not welcome in Chiang-Ri."

"So what will you do now?" Hongmin asked.

"What *can* we do? We go back to the river. At least there I can fish. I will look for a place near the water that no one has claimed. I will build some sort of shelter and maybe we can survive."

Hongmin looked over at his wife. Even in the flickering light from the fire he could see Li-Hua wiping tears from her eyes. He knew what she was feeling; Li-Hua had a soft heart and as poor as her family was, she still felt bad for those who were even less fortunate.

Hongmin turned back to the young couple and spoke, "Now that you have eaten, you must stay in our camp tonight and rest; then leave for the river in the morning."

CHAPTER NINE

Sichuan Province, China 2570 BC
Arrival Day

HALF OF THE CREW OF EIGHT sustained serious injuries in the "controlled crash" that brought the third scout ship down near the village in the Bayan Har Mountains. It was not the intended destination.

Six months before the mother ship was to enter earth orbit, the IMP Drive was restarted to provide reverse thrust that would slowly decelerate the ship from near-light speed to a velocity and direction suitable to achieve a sustainable earth orbit. The maneuver was accomplished flawlessly and without incident.

During the next three days the surface of the earth was carefully mapped and scanned for signs of advanced intelligent life. They detected no electromagnetic emissions and the optical telescope — capable of resolving objects the size of a large building — revealed no "organized" cities, but there was evidence of smaller settlements at several locations on the planetary surface. Very encouraging.

Based upon the analysis of the gathered data, the three scout ships were dispatched. The lead vessel successfully landed near Tiwanaku, in the foothills of the Andes in what is now modern day Bolivia. A second — in the Jordan Valley, near the Dead Sea. The intended destination for the third ship was the west coast of Africa, near what is now the Gola East Forest Reserve in Sierra Leone, and nearly at the midpoint between the other two landing sites. But a system failure occurred just as the third ship left earth orbit and began its descent. Navigational control was disrupted and not restored until the craft overshot the intended destination by several thousand kilometers.

The commander of the mother ship watched the path of the third vessel until it vanished from his sensor displays and all communication was lost. It was incorrectly concluded that the ship and her crew had been destroyed — crashing to earth or burning up in the atmosphere.

THE MEDICAL OFFICER ABOARD THE THIRD scout ship sustained only a few bruises in the crash and spent the next several hours caring for the four most seriously injured fellow crew members: one with a broken arm, one broken ankle, a scalp laceration with concussion, and a hand nearly severed with that crewman losing a great deal of blood. The Medical Officer was a skilled surgeon and was able to reattach the hand in less than four hours with one of the technicians pressed into service to assist.

In addition to the failure of the navigation system that was the cause of the crash, several other systems in the scouting craft were damaged upon impact. Most significant—and most frustrating to the Scout Ship Commander—was loss of the communication system. Without it, they would be unable to contact the mother ship or use it as a communication link to the other two landed scout vessels. The Commander concluded that it was doubtful that the mother ship knew where on the surface they had crashed or even that there were any survivors.

Before leaving orbit, the survey conducted from the mother ship confirmed that the surface temperature at the three intended landing sites was "in the range" of temperatures in the habitable regions of their home planet. Oxygen made up about 21% of the atmosphere—a slightly higher percentage than their home planet—and with insignificant levels of toxic gases. The gravitational force was about fifteen percent greater, consistent with the fact that the home planet was slightly less massive with an equatorial diameter about seven percent less.

BETWEEN THE MEDICAL EMERGENCIES and damage control after the crash landing, the crew gave scant attention to the surroundings outside their ship in the two hours before darkness set in.

But all of the crew members were up early the next morning, waiting for sunrise to see for themselves what kind of external environment they had been thrust into. The scene from the forward viewport and video images from the two sides and rear of the craft were far from spectacular. This location seemed particularly desolate with plenty of sand and rock and little vegetation. More than one of the crew members felt a sinking feeling in the stomach upon reflection that this place might become their permanent home.

But as the sun rose and the sky brightened, the environment outside did not appear quite so bleak. They began to see some animal life — lizards, rabbits, ground squirrels and a variety of birds. The crew members were excited because the animals they observed were not markedly different from similar species on their home planet.

By mid-morning, their excitement had given way to astonishment when they watched as a group of five clothed, biped inhabitants of the planet cautiously approach the scout ship. What astonished them was that with the exception of their dress and one or two physical attributes, these beings were indistinguishable from citizens from some of the southern Enclaves of their home planet.

The most distinguishing physical difference was that all of these beings possessed four fingers and an opposable thumb on each hand instead of a thumb and just three fingers. Similarly, their feet had five toes each instead of just four. A secondary distinction was that all five seemed somewhat "thicker" in the body; not overweight, but just not as slender as the typical citizen from home. The medical officer suggested that maybe the inhabitants had a more developed muscular system due to the greater gravitational force on this planet.

One of the females in the crew posed the question, *"What do you think is the purpose of the extra toes and fingers?"* But none of her crewmates offered a plausible explanation.

As the entities outside came closer to the scout vessel, unaware that they were being observed from inside the craft, every uttered word and phrase was being recorded by the vessel's system data loggers. Not surprisingly, the crew's Linguistics Specialist was able to categorically state that the language being spoken outside was dissimilar to every known spoken language from their home planet. The ship's computer system was designed to separate the voice tracks of each individual speaker. Sophisticated speech recognition software would be used to build a vocabulary database of this unknown language so that soon it would be possible to engage in rudimentary communication with the "locals," as they came to be called by the crew members.

By mid-afternoon, several more groups of locals had come to see the strange object that had appeared outside their village. One group even included a male chieftain of sorts, judging by the manner in which he seemed to be treated with signs of deference and attention from the locals who

accompanied him. After approaching the vessel —
maintaining a respectable distance — he stopped
until all eyes were upon him, then waved his arms
and with a commanding voice addressed the locals,
making what seemed to the crew inside the ship to
be an important announcement or directive. Shortly
afterwards, most of locals left the area, following
behind the chief and his entourage.

By evening, when no other locals had come near
the ship since the departure of the chief, the entire
crew met to discuss when and how to best initiate a
face-to-face encounter with the local population. The
Linguistics Specialist reported that the speech
recognition application had created a vocabulary of
about 150 words and phrases used by the locals. She
demonstrated the two-way wrist translator that she
had previously loaded with the vocabulary database
file. She spoke a phrase in her native language, then
passed her free hand over the translator and it
repeated the phrase in the local language. She then
spoke a phrase unintelligible to the crew in the local
language, passed her hand over the translator, and
it repeated the phrase in the crew's home language.

The crew was favorably impressed with the
two-way translation demonstration. Over the next
hour, the Commander of the ship outlined a plan for
the next day to make contact and attempt to
communicate with one or more of the locals.

THE CREW WAS AWAKENED before daylight by
a clanging sound. The video monitor showed four of

the locals wielding a long metal bar, apparently attempting to pry open the access port on the side of the craft. It was unlikely that their efforts would enable them to gain entry to the ship, but the damage might render the port inoperable, making it impossible for the crew to exit without first dismantling the port mechanism from the inside. The Commander quickly ordered the crew to activate the exterior lighting and the emergency alarm. The action had the desired result. The four locals immediately stopped their activity and retreated to a safe distance away from the craft.

The Commander had planned for an encounter with the locals for later that day, but the attempted forced entry persuaded him that there was no better time than the present. He first secured the alarm, then ordered that the port be opened. The response outside was immediate: the gang of four retreated a few steps further back and crowded in close to each other, senses alerted for any new activity from the ship. When the two strangely-dressed figures emerged from the port, one of the four raised the metal bar and assumed a defensive stance.

The Commander and the Linguistics Specialist stopped just outside the ship, facing the locals. Each raised their right hand with open palm, in hopes of signaling their peaceful intentions. The Linguistics Specialist was wearing the two-way translator on her wrist, but before exiting the ship the Commander had asked if she had learned enough to initiate a verbal greeting in the local language. She obliged. "We are visitors from far away. We mean you no harm. We bring greetings." The Commander hoped for a peaceful encounter, but carried a side arm—holstered and strapped to his waist—just in case.

One of the four locals slowly stepped forward, raised his right hand in like manner, and spoke. "Where are you from and what do you want?" The words came out of the translation device.

"We come from the stars." The last word in the sentence came out without translation as there was as yet no equivalent word in the language database. The Commander gazed upward, parroting the words from the translator, "We come from the stars," pointing to the sky with his index finger, "and we seek only peace and friendship."

The local replied, "Greetings. My name is Hongmin."

CHAPTER TEN

ROGER ATWOOD and Amanda Marshall returned to Melanie's suite in Alexandria for a second day of briefing from her father concerning Professor Chu and the Dropa Stones.

"How was it, Professor, that you began your academic collaboration with Professor Chu?" Amanda had placed her voice recorder on the marble coffee table.

"His very first lecture at University in Beijing— I found it most interesting, especially when he described the Dropa Stones and nearly invisible symbols engraved in the surface. He tell us that it was a graduate student at Chengdu who first discovered the engravings while examining the surface of one disc under microscope. There was a spiral groove in each of the discs that could be seen with unaided eye, but the engraved symbols— characters that made up the inscription at bottom of each groove—became visible only under high magnification."

"Could you describe the inscriptions and symbols, Professor?"

"In his lecture, Professor Chu tell us that the inscriptions were maybe fifteen hundred characters long, each made up using combinations of some forty different character symbols. The symbols were made up using straight and curved lines, some geometric shapes."

"I am totally ignorant on the subject of written languages," offered Roger, "but from what you are describing, it sounds as if the forty characters were the equivalent of an alphabet, used to make up individual words in the inscriptions. Is that correct?"

"Yes, that was conclusion made by Professor Chu's graduate student at Chengdu." Roger seemed mildly embarrassed by the Professor's statement: Clearly, it didn't take a Ph.D. to conclude that the characters represented an alphabet. Amanda raised her hand to her mouth to cover the wisp of a smile on her face. "But after two year of study, the Professor's department at Chengdu make no progress at translating inscriptions. So the Administration send one disc to Peking and another to University in Moscow. Research work at Chengdu stopped with disruption from war and never resumed after Communist Revolution.

"I meet with Professor Chu right after his lecture. We talk together late into the night during that first meeting. When he learned of my work breaking codes during the war and linguistics research, he suggest that maybe I could work on translating the inscriptions. It was difficult because I have my own research as well as teaching responsibility, but it was a challenge I could not turn down. Professor Chu and I work with transcriptions of the symbol characters found on discs for more than two years."

"Can we see what the symbols actually looked like; can you show us?" Amanda posed the question to Professor Tsum.

"I have much to show you." He addressed Melanie, "Daughter, would you bring the carry-on travel bag from my room? It is in the back of my closet." Melanie Tsum rose quickly and retrieved the bag from her father's bedroom and handed to him. He removed a three-ring binder from the bag and opened the cover. From the pouch on the inside of the front cover he removed two large black and white photographs and placed them on top of one another on the marble table. "This is photograph of small portion of one disc near the central perforation. The curved line that you see is a section of the spiral groove, and this —" he pointed to a dark semi-circular area cut off by the edge of the print. "This is the central perforation. This print is a three-times magnification of the actual size of the disc."

"The groove looks like a black line — no detail," Roger noted.

"Yes, because the lighting makes shadow, and not close enough. But this other photograph shows more detail." Professor Tsum lifted the first photo, revealing the second. The magnification was greater and the improved illumination revealed the symbols engraved at the bottom of the groove. The symbols appeared to be grouped together with a dot (·) between groups, or in some case a double dot (· ·). The groups themselves were of various lengths, from a single character to strings of a dozen or more. "And you will notice that the uniformity and small size of the symbols suggest that they were machine generated — obviously not made by hand work."

"So, Professor, would it be incorrect to assume that —" Roger paused momentarily, " — that the single dots separate words and the double dots signify the start of a new sentence or paragraph?"

"Well, yes, that was our conclusion. But at this time we did not know even the direction in which the characters should to be read." Amanda had a quizzical expression on her face. Professor Tsum explained, "Most Western languages are written from left to right, but there are some that read from right to left, as is the case for Arabic, Hebrew and some Asian languages. The inscriptions on the disc in Beijing appeared as a single string, but it took several weeks before we determine that the direction of writing in the groove was from central perforation in direction outward along the spiral to the edge." Professor Tsum snapped open the metal rings of the binder, removed two sheets of narrow-ruled notebook paper and placed the sheets on the marble table. "These pages represent the string of characters transcribed from the Dropa disc that I had in my possession—the disc that is hopefully safely on way here from Bangkok."

Roger picked up the pages and passed one of them to Amanda to examine. The handwritten sheets were faded and yellowed with age. "And you were able to decipher this inscription? How long did it take?"

"Yes. Well—more or less. It take two years."

"And the translation? What does it say?"

"Here, Professor Atwood." Professor Tsum handed Roger a folded sheet of paper. "That is English translation of the text from a paper that Professor Chu and I publish in 1956. I prepare the English translation during my flight from Bangkok." Roger read it aloud for Amanda's benefit:

WE WERE SPACE TRAVELERS. WE NUMBER MANY WHO DEPARTED OUR PLANET IN THE 77TH YEAR OF THE UNITED GOVERNMENT. WE SPEAK LONG LIFE, WISDOM AND JOY TO THE ELECTED RULERS OF OUR PLANET.

WE FOUND THIS PLACE MUCH SIMILAR TO OUR OWN. BUT OUR STAR IS SO DISTANT THAT EVEN THE LIGHT MUST WAIT MANY YEARS TO ARRIVE HERE. LOOK IN THE SKY NEAR THE GROUP OF STARS THAT YOU KNOW AS 'BEAK OF THE TURTLE' AND YOU WILL KNOW FROM WHERE WE COME.

EIGHT OF US COME TO THESE MOUNTAINS CARRIED IN A SMALL CRAFT BROKEN ON ARRIVAL. WE MAKE MANY FRIENDSHIPS WITH THE LOCAL BEINGS WHO CALL THEMSELVES THE DROPA. THEY ARE IN MOST WAYS IN THE BODY SIMILAR TO US. WE TEACH THE DROPA MUCH ABOUT GROWING FOOD AND MAKING TOOLS FROM METALLIC SUBSTANCE. MANY TOOLS HAVE BEEN MADE FROM PARTS OF THE BROKEN CRAFT THAT BROUGHT US HERE.

WE THE EIGHT LEARNED THE SPOKEN TONGUE OF THE DROPA BUT THEY HAVE NO WRITTEN LANGUAGE. WE HELP THE DROPA SO THEY CAN HAVE A WRITTEN LANGUAGE OF THEIR OWN. WE ALSO TEACH THEM THE LAW OF NUMBERS IN THEIR OWN CUSTOM OF THE RULE OF ZOM.

BUT AMONG THE DROPA THERE WERE ALSO SOME WHO HELD HATE AND DISTRUST IN THEIR HEARTS. THEY ATTACKED AND MURDERED THE FIVE OF US WHOSE REMAINS LIE IN THIS PLACE.

TO ALL WHO ARE ABLE TO READ THIS: KNOW THAT YOU HAVE GROWN MUCH AS A PEOPLE BUT THERE ARE MORE SECRETS LOCKED WITHIN WAITING TO BE DISCOVERED.

TO ALL WHO ARE ABLE TO READ THIS: KNOW ALSO THAT THE CREATOR OF OUR PLANET AND LIFE UPON IT AS WRITTEN IN OUR ANCIENT SACRED SCROLLS IS THE SELFSAME CREATOR OF THIS WORLD AND OF THE UNIVERSE.

Roger was silent for nearly a minute after completing the reading. He raised one hand to his brow as he silently reread the words on the paper. "I don't know exactly what to say. To me, this is a very moving message. If we can believe that it was written by visitors thousands of years ago, we must accept that it was intended for modern humans, like us." Amanda nodded slowly, in agreement. Melanie was beaming; obviously proud of her father's work.

"I am sorry," offered Professor Tsum, "that some of sentence structure is awkward. I am not so fluent with English translation from our paper. It was published in Traditional Chinese, and some parts even in my language were difficult. For example, the part about the 'Law of Numbers' is clearly meaning 'Mathematics,' but we never could understand the phrase 'Rule of Zom.' There is no meaning of that word in Chinese."

"I have a question." Amanda spoke as she took the paper from Roger's hands. "What is meant by 'Beak of the Turtle'?"

"I can answer that," offered Melanie. "The *Beak of the Turtle* is a constellation from ancient Chinese astronomy and astrology—a grouping of a few stars at the head of Orion, the Hunter. But what do you think, Father, is the meaning of the challenge near the end of the translation—about unlocking the secrets within? Within the disc?"

"Professor Chu and I spend long hours pondering that question. Before our paper was final published in Beijing, the Engineering Department at our university performed analysis on disc to see what might be learned about material properties. Similar analysis done at Chengdu did not produce any useful result, but at Beijing, they learn that the disc material is a metal alloy combined with ceramic. Very unusual. The alloy was iron, nickel and cobalt. The edge of the disc has a thick clear ceramic coating, but x-ray images show nothing unusual—just a uniform metal-ceramic structure throughout inside of the disc."

"What about the other Dropa Stone discs and the inscriptions on them?" Roger posed the question.

"The disc that Professor Chu and I study was one that was sent to Beijing years earlier. We had little information about the others—the discs left at Chengdu and one that was sent to Soviet Union. This, of course, is what Professor Chu told me; I have never seen any of the other discs. When we make inquiries, we were told that the discs had been misplaced and could not be found. While at Chengdu, Professor Chu had made some notes that included partial transcriptions from one of the missing discs. It appeared to have the same sequence of symbols as disc that I study. Existence of five discs was mentioned in our paper published in 1956, but it is not known if all five discs had identical inscriptions. We hoped to publish a follow-up paper if any of the other missing discs could be found." Professor Tsum retrieved several pages printed in Chinese from his bag and handed them to Roger.

"This, I take it, is your original paper?" Professor Tsum nodded. "If it included your deciphered message from the—" Roger paused, "—from the space travelers, it must have immediately created quite a stir in the academic community."

"It would seem to be so, but in truth there was little initial response. We publish in a journal that was not widely circulated. Finally, when translations in English and German were made available, it did generate much interest, but not from scientific community. Instead, it was referenced by many pseudo-scientists who were interested only in big profits from sales of books about ancient astronauts.

"The Administration at our university was unhappy about the bad publicity. We were told that we had brought dishonor to the school. Our research grant was suspended and they tell Professor Chu that he could no longer teach after end of the current term. But even before the end of the term, he told me that he expected to be arrested any day. Less than one week later he was gone.

"I was allowed to remain at the University, but lost my position as Department Head. I was forbidden to conduct any further research concerning the Dropa Stones. I knew that university or government officials would soon try to confiscate the disc that I had studied, so I took it to my home and buried it under the floor. When I was asked about it, I told them it must be with the other missing discs. For the next few years I try to avoid all controversy as I have much concern for my family, but always I believed that the government was watching me.

"It was unhappy time for me with much bad luck. But my bad luck turns much worse when Red Guards come to the university."

"Yes, I've read about the time of the Red Guards in China," Roger added, "and about the Cultural Revolution."

CHAPTER ELEVEN

Guangling, near Beijing, China
1966

THE SOVIET UNION WAS THE CHIEF supporter of the fledgling Chinese government after the Communist takeover in 1949. During the next seven years Moscow sent financial aid as well as an army of 15,000 engineers and technicians to help China along the road to industrialization. Ideologues in both countries heralded the huge infusion of support, anxious to prove to the world that Communism was clearly superior to any other economic model.

But by 1955, Mao and other hardliners in China looked upon the few recent liberal reforms instituted in the Soviet Union as violations of the principles of Lenin, Marx and Stalin. Nikita Khrushchev, who had supported some of the reforms, assumed power after Stalin's death in 1953. Mao rejected any thought of straying from original Party principles and relations between the two countries became strained. The Soviet engineers and technicians went home, leaving hundreds of unfinished projects across China without the technical human resources needed to see them through to completion.

Mao and his supporters argued that industrialization could proceed without foreign help, relying solely on Communist principles and the hard work of the Chinese people. It became known as the "Great Leap Forward." Officials called for the peasants in recently reorganized collectives to operate "backyard blast furnaces," melting down scrap iron and broken tools and utensils for the production of steel. Production quotas were established, but in most cases, there was insufficient available scrap to meet the quota and the metal that was produced was often of inferior quality. In order to avoid the wrath of their superiors for failing to meet quotas and lack of quality, members of the collectives throughout the country began to melt down any available metal, including serviceable plows, shovels and other useful tools. Food shortages became common as labor was diverted from agriculture to support steel production and similar industrialization projects. The Great Leap Forward was an abject failure, but those who dared speak against it were denounced as traitors.

By 1960 the government officials in charge — including Chairman Mao — were ready to abandon the failed initiative. Mao agreed to turn management of the economy over to more experienced men. Within five years, the team of

Deng Xiaoping, Liu Shaoqi and Zhou Enlai was able to successfully grow the economy.

During this period, Mao stepped away from his position of visible power in politics and government. He devoted much time to study and writing, but watched with concern as his former supporters who now held the reins of power seemed determined to follow a more liberal economic policy patterned after the Soviet economic evolution. He understood that his return to power and fundamental principles could occur only by overthrowing the present Party leadership.

Mao was still revered by the population as the Father of Modern China, but at age seventy-two, he needed to prove that he was capable of taking back overall control of the government. To this end, Mao created a special media event with himself as the star, taking a swim in the Yangtze River in 1966 to show that he was still physically fit.

Mao delivered a number of speeches at Party events and large public gatherings criticizing Party leadership for touting Western economic theories and elitist attitudes and separating themselves from the Proletariat. He praised the small groups of students known as the Red Guards who had taken it upon themselves to identify and discourage any capitalist notions and anti-Maoist ideas that they encountered as they swept through small towns and villages near Beijing. Schools were closed throughout the country so that hundreds of thousands of eager high school and university students could join the ranks of the Red Guards, giving rise to the movement that became known as the Cultural Revolution.

The members of Mao's former team of three were removed from power, but only Liu Shaoqi was imprisoned, where he was beaten and later died. The Red Guards took pleasure in seeking out professionals and the well-educated — individuals who tended toward anti-Maoist thinking — and relocating them to collective farms away from the cities.

THE RED GUARD GROUP LEADER was barely twenty years old, yet he commanded the undivided attention of his Red Guard comrades as well as the assemblage of new arrivals from the city.

"We welcome you to the collective here at Guangling. For your time here, you will find a simpler life than many of you may have become accustomed. This life is consistent with the words of our Great Leader who said 'The principle of diligence and frugality should be observed in everything.' While you are here, you will work hard and study hard. The study will encompass many of the principles that our Great Revolution brought forth. Each of you will be given one of these." The Group Leader held up a copy of the "Little Red Book," *Quotations from Chairman Mao Tse-Tung*, for all to see. "By the time you leave this place and return to your homes, you will know by heart many of the sayings of truth found in this book."

Tsum looked over at the man seated cross-legged on the ground next to him. He was a colleague—an instructor in Professor Tsum's Department. When the Red Guards had come to the University two days earlier, they ordered most of the staff whose names appeared on a prepared list to assemble on the soccer field. After a brief speech explaining that they had been selected for a new government initiative aimed at re-education, they were taken in groups of two or three to one of several staging areas where they would join with other professionals—doctors, lawyers and businessmen—from the city. From there, groups of twenty or more were sent by truck or bus to one of the many collective farms up to one hundred miles from the city.

The Red Guard leader continued, "Here at the collective, we recognize that many of you bring special skills from your previous education and training. When it comes to work assignments, it is in the interest of the State that we match your skills with the available work. I am told that we have two esteemed individuals among us who were members of the faculty at the University in Beijing. Would the two of you please step forward, so that we can recognize your achievements?"

Professor Tsum and his protégé rose slowly, stepped to the front and stood next to the Red Guard Group Leader. Neither of the men was smiling. The Group Leader continued, referring to his notes, "This is Professor Tsum from the Anthropology

Department at the University, and Lin Baio, an instructor in the same department. Please tell us, Professor, something of your work at the University."

"I specialize in ancient Chinese language and writing." He spoke softly, not raising his eyes to the men seated in front of him.

"Louder, please, Professor; so that all might hear you."

"I conduct research and teach the students about early Chinese language and writing; from before the first Dynasty."

"And can you tell us, Professor, how your work has helped further the vision of Chairman Mao for our Great Revolution?"

"I believe it is important to know where we came from, in order to guide us to our future."

"Well said, Professor." The Red Guard Group Leader turned to one his assistants. "Please bring the tools that the Professor and his protégé will be using in their important new work assignment here at the collective." The assistant handed each of the two men a shovel. "Because of the prestigious position that you held at the University, you have been assigned to work with the livestock here at the collective. For the next two weeks, you shall be cleaning the hog pens." The group of seated men laughed as the Leader's assistant led Professor Tsum and Instructor Baio off in the direction toward the livestock pens. "Now," the Group Leader turned his attention back to the group of men seated before him, "do we have any physicians among us?"

AFTER THE FIRST WEEK, the new conscripts at the collective had become familiar with the schedule: work assignment for ten hours a day, six days each week; instruction two hours each evening after work, four hours of instruction on the seventh day. The mid-day meal consisted of rice and vegetables. In the evening, it was the same except for the addition of a small portion of chicken or pork.

The ten hog pens at the collective each held six mature animals and their piglets. Professor Tsum and Lin Baio worked together cleaning the pens. One of them would transport two buckets full of pig manure to a nearby ox cart and dump them while the other filled two more buckets with his shovel. The buckets were carried in pairs by one man, suspending them from the ends of a stout bamboo shoulder yoke. When the cart was full, they would together drive it out to the planting fields, some 200 meters away, emptying each load in a separate pile adjacent to the fields.

Lin Baio posed a question as they transported what would be their last delivery for the day, late in the afternoon. "Professor, each day we bring many loads of pig shit to these fields, but the next day the piles are mostly gone. Do they really use all of it to fertilize these crops?"

"Yes, they do. And they recently started using much more of it."

"Because?"

"Because the Party Agriculture Committee decided that it would be possible to greatly increase the crop yield per hectare by doubling the planting density. The close planting requires more nutrients."

"That sounds like a good idea. Chairman Mao would be pleased by such initiative."

"It is folly. Professor from the Agriculture Department told me that the close planting causes the plants to strangle each other, so the yields are even less than before."

CHAPTER TWELVE

Sichuan Province, China
18 Months after the Arrival

THE LAST YEAR AND ONE-HALF since the arrival of the Visitors represented a distinctly positive period for *most* of the local inhabitants in the Bayan Har Mountains. The Visitors had done much to improve the lives of the locals. They were taught improved planting techniques, and an irrigation system was built to bring water to the new crop fields. Some of the exterior panels of the Visitor's space craft had been removed to fashion agricultural implements. The crew's Linguistics Specialist was able to develop a simple written alphabet based on the speech sounds of the local language. She organized and taught some classes for several of the local children who showed special promise.

Although the crew of the scout craft fully understood that their damaged vessel would never leave the surface of the planet, they were still optimistic about their chances to join up with their fellow explorers and eventually complete the mission and return to their home planet.

Many of the ship's subsystems had been damaged or degraded, and the crew worked diligently to maintain the critically important computer system as well as the solar array and battery bank that provided power to it. The computer system still contained a copy of the survey data and maps that had been recorded by the mother ship before the three scout ships left earth orbit. With this information and the computerized video recording of their disastrous descent to the surface, they were able to mark their present position on the maps to within thirty kilometers. Knowing their approximate location was the good news. The bad news was that 3,000 kilometers of mostly difficult terrain separated them from the designated landing point of the second scout ship — the present location of their nearest fellow explorers.

Due to the extreme distance, an overland expedition to the landing site of the second scout ship was quickly dismissed as an unreasonable option, but the Commander acknowledged that exploring some closer locations could prove scientifically useful. Since their arrival, the Geology Specialist and a technician assistant had completed several three and four-day trips up to forty kilometers from the crash site. Now they proposed a far more ambitious mission: from the survey maps they identified a lake and adjacent village in a valley surrounded by a chain of mountains. The map images suggested the presence of a community that had been laid out in an intelligent manner; perhaps indicative of a more advanced culture than they had seen in the local population.

It would not be an easy journey. The proposed destination was more than 300 kilometers distant. On the day of their departure, the Commander issued only one order to the pair of crew members — the male Geology Specialist and female technician — making the trip, "You are to complete your journey and return to our location within two lunar cycles — fifty-nine days."

LANDON, THE COMMUNICATIONS OFFICER from the ship had spent most of his spare time since the arrival attempting to repair the high frequency radio transmitter and receiver that had been damaged in the crash. The crew had been able to neither send to nor receive transmissions from the mother ship — the bright star-like object that they could still see in the night sky — passing overhead every ninety minutes. And although his repair efforts had proved futile, he nonetheless remained undaunted. Now, instead of attempting to repair the old communication system, he would work on building a new one, cannibalizing parts from the ship that he could press into service. One of the locals had volunteered to help him.

"I APPRECIATE YOUR HELP, Hongmin." The Communications Officer had been struggling to raise a three-meter long pine log and drop one end into a hole he had dug a few meters away from the ship. With the local man's assistance, they were able to set this post into the ground, packing the earth around the base with their feet. A second post was raised in similar fashion on the other side of the ship. The posts would support the ends of two wires strung from the ship in opposite directions, forming a simple dipole antenna. The COM Officer had scavenged the wire from the ship's lighting system.

"I am happy to help, Landon, but I still do not understand how these wooden posts and wire will help you hear the voice of your friends from far away." The COM Officer considered for a moment how he could possibly answer the question without inviting even more questions.

"You will have to just wait and see. When I have it working, you can come and listen for yourself." Minutes before, Hongmin had been standing on Landon's shoulders for the benefit of the extra height, tacking the wire to the top of the second post—as he had been directed—with a large metal staple and hammer. Now safely back on the ground, they stood together, looking up and surveying their finished work. "Thank you, again. I have more work to do later, but now I'm hungry. You must be hungry as well. Let's find something to eat."

Not too far from the crippled ship, the crew had finished construction of a covered gazebo-like structure a few weeks after their arrival. During good weather, it served as a gathering place for meals and relaxation with tables and chairs and a raised cooking hearth located downwind according to the prevailing breezes. The covered area was more than six meters square and included a flagstone floor. Pine log posts supported the shingled roof.

The COM Officer grabbed two apples from a carved wooden bowl and tossed one to his guest. Near the hearth, he found several overdone cuts of rabbit in a covered metal pan. They were leftovers from the previous evening meal. While the two men sat and ate, a young stray dog approached very slowly, stopped a few meters away and laid down, facing the men. When Landon noticed the animal he rose and slowly moved toward it, holding out a cut of the roast meat. He stopped a meter away from it and spoke in a soft voice, encouraging the animal to come forward and take the meat from his hand. The dog began to whimper, afraid to come closer. Finally, the animal's fear was overcome by his hunger and he scooched toward Landon with his belly dragging the ground all the way. The young dog grabbed the meat from Landon's hand and quickly retreated with his prize.

"Why are you feeding that feral animal?" Hongmin asked. "You will never be rid of him."

"I know, Hongmin. He has been coming here every evening for the last week, and I always give him a little meat."

"But why? It is just a useless animal."

"Maybe. I see the dogs that run in packs from time to time, but this one is different. He is always alone. We have no similar animals on my home planet. Many keep animals for companionship, similar to your rabbits and cats, but this dog seems far more intelligent. I believe he could be a loyal friend and companion to me if I can win him over." By now the dog had finished his meal and disappeared into the woods.

"I still do not understand, but if it pleases you to keep this animal as a pet, then it pleases me also."

"Thank you. Now I have a question for you, Hongmin."

"Yes."

"You know that we have tried very hard to be good neighbors to your people."

"Yes, we know. You have taught us much, and your doctor has helped many who were sick. For the first time, we are able to raise our children without fear for their health."

"We have met most of the people from your village; many we know by name. Almost all of your people are friendly with us — except for your chief. We have met with him just once for a short time. After that, he does not accept our invitations. We have sent gifts, but he refuses them. Our Commander wants to have friendly relations with your chief, if we can. What can be done?"

"I know of the problem. I think it is not so much with the chief, but with Zhang Zhu, his son, and friends of the son."

"Why? What is the problem?"

"The Chief is old. Maybe it is not too long before Zhang Zhu becomes the new Chief. But everyone in the village knows that the Chief has lost much power and control since you arrive here. In the past, the village people would look to our Chief for counsel and help, but no longer. Now they come to you and other Visitors. Zhu believes he may someday be chief with no people to rule. The Soothsayer has warned him so. This also makes his friends unhappy. They would be important and share power with Zhu, but not now. Not since you and the other Visitors have come."

"I see."

Hongmin continued, "You must be careful. Zhang Zhu is very jealous, and he and his friends can be dangerous." As the COM Officer paused to consider Hongmin's warning, a female crew member stepped down from the ship and nodded and smiled as she walked past the two men and grabbed an apple from the bowl. Hongmin turned to watch as she returned to the ship and disappeared inside. "Now, I have a question for you, my friend."

"What is it, Hongmin?"

"With four men and four women in your crew, our village women spend much time gossiping about you. I have heard it myself. Are you especially close with one or more of the women in your crew?"

The COM Officer laughed, "Why do you ask, Hongmin?"

"I mean no disrespect. Whenever I see the sister of my wife, she asks about you. Her name is Jia-Li. Her husband died in the year before you arrive. He went hunting on the mountain for the sheep with the big horn." Hongmin pointed to one of the mountain peaks in the distance to the north, "And he fell from a high place and died. She has been alone for a long time. Maybe you can meet and speak with her someday. She would like that, I think."

"Maybe I can."

"I think she is very beautiful—maybe more beautiful than my wife. She is younger and has no children." Hongmin smiled broadly before continuing. "But maybe you won't think she is beautiful because she has too many fingers and toes."

The COM Officer laughed out loud at his friend's teasing remark.

CHAPTER THIRTEEN

The Jordan Valley
Arrival Day

THE SECOND SCOUT SHIP landed without incident in an arid region of the planet near a large lake fed from a river to the south. That location had been selected because proximity to fresh water increased the likelihood that a wider variety of plant and animal life might be found and studied. The analysts who had reviewed the survey data gathered aboard the mother ship judged that the much larger sea lying about 100 kilometers to the west likely had a high saline concentration and so the lake region — they surmised — would be more hospitable to life. The analysts couldn't have been more wrong.

The survey team of three crew members sent to gather samples were able to hike to the water's edge and return in less than an hour. Plant life was scarce anywhere near the lake and the only animal species they found were ants on the limbs of scrawny trees and rabbit-like ground squirrels inhabiting rock outcroppings. The ship's laboratory was able to provide an explanation: the salt content of the water was incredibly high at thirty percent — far too high for aquatic plants or animals. Serious consideration was given to abandoning the region entirely and relocating the scout ship. The final decision was made by the mother ship Commander. He ordered that the scout ship remain at the present location for several weeks of exploration and study before moving on to a more promising location.

The crew members were enthusiastic about the reports from the first scout ship — reports that had been relayed to them by the mother ship. It had landed in the foothills of the Andes Mountains in what is now modern day Bolivia, near the border with Peru. The reports included numerous accounts of friendly encounters with the local population. It was particularly gratifying to hear that the four or five nearby communities were at peace with one another and had been for generations; this despite the fact that they appeared to be independently governed with no higher level authority.

When asked what might account for this pleasantly unexpected finding, the crew members discovered that the leaders within the independent villages routinely met together to discuss and solve common problems. They were able agree on an equitable sharing of water rights, and were generous in sharing their stores of food during times of drought and famine. No doubt the leadership's practice of encouraging intermarriage between members of the different villages helped maintain lines of communication and promoted the notion of peaceful cooperation.

And so the crew of the second ship looked forward with high expectations to their first encounter with the local inhabitants of the Jordan Valley. But as the days passed they became frustrated with their inability to make any meaningful connection with the locals. They observed several nomadic herdsmen with their flocks — groups of several individuals that appeared at first to be approaching their location, only to see them abruptly change direction after becoming aware of the presence of the scout ship and their encampment.

After the third week the Commander of the scout ship reluctantly concluded that any chance encounter that might lead to meaningful communication with the local inhabitants was highly unlikely. At a meeting of the crew members it was decided to send the three-member scouting party to the walled city about fifteen kilometers north of their location.

They had seen a glimpse of the city on approach to their landing site. The plan was to leave the next morning and carry provisions for two days. So as to appear less threatening to the locals, they prepared and wore apparel similar to what they had observed as typical dress of the passing herdsmen. The travel and hoped for encounter with the local population might be risky, so side arms would be issued to all three members of the scouting party.

BY LATE MORNING the walled city first came into view. It had taken three hours to traverse the slowly rising terrain leading to the plateau on which the city had been built. As they came closer they observed some excited activity in the parapet above the wall on one side of the wooden gate.

The scouting party stopped about thirty meters directly in front of the gate. From this location, they had to look up to the parapet. In just a few minutes, the number of individuals looking down upon them had doubled, as had the volume of chatter coming from above. The leader of the three asked his companions for their opinion of the situation.

"It doesn't appear that they are about to welcome us and invite us in."

"I agree," replied another team member. "Maybe we should rethink this."

"Let's wait and see what happens next." The team leader unconsciously felt for the weapon under his garment. He activated his wrist-mounted two-way translator. It would be of no help interpreting the speech of the locals during this first encounter, but recording the communication would begin the process of building a language vocabulary for any future encounters.

One of the older men in the parapet seemed to be in charge—an elder of the city. His black robe was trimmed in bright red and he wore a large puffy hat that partially concealed his ears. He gestured for quiet to the men around him, then shouted down to the three strangers, "Where are you from, and what do you want?" The words were unintelligible to the travelers, but the meaning was predictable in light of the circumstances.

The team leader stepped forward, spread open his arms and hands as a peaceful gesture, and shouted back, "We are travelers who come in peace. May we have permission to enter your city?"

The volume of the chatter rose as the men in the parapet grew increasingly agitated. One man moved within inches of the elder's face, pleading with him as he pointed to his own open left hand. "Did you not see the stranger's hands?" The man shouted at the elder, "It is the mark of the Devil." Without waiting for further word from the elder, the men in the parapet began shouting at the travelers, then rained down stones in their direction from the piles of same stored in the parapet for that purpose.

Most of the thrown missiles fell short, but the travelers made the prudent decision to move further away from the angry crowd. The fusillade continued until four loud reports suddenly rang out. The source of the startling noise was a sidearm pointed in the sky by the leader of the scouting party. The four shots disintegrated four of the many incoming missiles directed at them.

A hush immediately came over the men in the parapet—a reaction to both the noise from the weapon and the impressive visual of rocks turned to harmless dust in midair. "Surely these are Devils," whispered the elder to the men who had crowded in close together, seeking sanctuary from the terror that they feared would soon befall them.

The auto-track and fire feature of the team leader's weapon had subdued the aggressive crowd for now, but the danger was still present. The team leader made the decision that they would leave the environs of the city and return to the scout ship.

Just as they reached the edge of the plateau and were about to proceed along the downward grade, they heard a shout from behind. They turned to see a man running in their direction and waving his arms. He had long hair and a full beard and wore a white flowing robe and sandals.

"Please wait. I must speak with you." He was out of breath, but smiled broadly when he reached the three. As he spoke, most of what they understood was from his gestures. "They called you Devils, but I do not believe it. I, too, was a stranger here many months ago. The people in this land are very unfriendly. They trust only their own people, believing that strangers will steal their goods and do them harm. I am sorry, but it was prudent for you to leave the city."

"We do not understand much of what you say, but we can tell from your countenance that you come to us in peace and friendship. We thank you for that." The leader of the three then pointed to himself and spoke his own name, "Randor." He then pointed to the man in the white robe. "What is your name?"

"Marlot. I am Marlot," replied the man in the white robe.

CHAPTER FOURTEEN

Home Planet of the Visitors
2556 BC

IT HAD BEEN TWENTY-NINE YEARS since the Star Ship set out on the historic mission into space. After so many years, there was special excitement in the land once again because it was the earliest opportunity to learn if the explorers of the Grand Expedition had succeeded in reaching the distant planet.

Years earlier, government scientists had become frustrated with their non-scientist citizens who seemed unable to understand why they hadn't already heard from the explorers. *Had the mission failed*, they asked?

Many citizens seemed unable to grasp the fact that the explorers had likely reached their destination nearly fifteen years earlier, but that it took until now — another fourteen years later — for the radio transmission report of that event to travel the 140 trillion kilometers back through space to the home planet. In fact, the scientists explained, if the explorers have completed their mission as planned, they would be home sometime within the next five years. The Star Ship would be following not far behind any radio messages that might be sent.

The whole matter had caused great confusion. The scientists were especially frustrated to learn that the consensus in many of the outlying "Third World" Enclaves (where most of the population was born after the mission began) was that the mission never actually took place. It was a hoax—they believed—perpetrated solely to justify large tax increases and government expenditures intended to somehow benefit the privileged classes, notably the Patricians.

But for most of the citizens of the home planet, the discussion and excitement over the much anticipated radio message from space was a welcome diversion. Much had changed in twenty-nine years, both politically and economically. The Union of Enclaves that represented the seventy-eight member states of the Unification Government had remained intact for more than one hundred years, but calls for dissolution of the government persisted—most frequently heard from leaders in the poorer Enclaves.

The promised new era of economic prosperity that would be ushered in by the investment and expenditure for the Grand Expedition never fully materialized and disappeared entirely within five years after the launch. Unification Government officials argued that the economy could be jumpstarted with the economic stimulus afforded by new government investment in infrastructure — roads, bridges, power plants, ports and airports — but the Treasury surplus that had funded the Grand Expedition years earlier had long ago been reduced to near zero.

From the first days of the establishment of the Unification Government and Constitution after the end of the Enclave Wars, there were tough but sound restrictions on government spending and the money supply. Paper currency and notes that represented the official monetary unit of exchange — the *Gildar* — were 100% backed by precious metals, notably gold and platinum. Some of the baser metals, like silver and copper that were used in electronics and construction, found their way into lower denomination coinage.

In the tenth year after the mission began the government sought to raise capital for the proposed new economic stimulus by offering bonds, but the low interest rate returns attracted few investors. And so the Treasury, under orders from the Administrators, issued a decree stating that Unification currency would no longer be fully backed by the precious metals stored in the Treasury vaults. Further, that all gold and platinum specie in the hands of citizens was to be turned in for exchange with paper currency of the same value. With the exception of jewelry or in medical and dental applications, citizens would henceforth be forbidden to hold gold or platinum in any form.

Now that the constraint requiring full backing for every new paper *Gildar* had been removed, the Treasury was free to print as much money as the new spending programs demanded.

WHEN THE LONG-AWAITED FIRST MESSAGE from the explorers of the Grand Expedition arrived, it was immediately flashed to every media outlet on the planet. It had been sent fourteen years earlier, just a few hours after the Star Ship had successfully achieved orbit around the distant planet. The message text itself was short, but included an image of the planet taken from the 160 kilometer high orbit. Most agreed that the image depicted the planet as a thing of great beauty, with white clouds and large expanses of deep blue ocean. This first message and the subsequent ones received every few days thereafter were uplifting to the population of the planet—citizens who had heard little in the way of good news for a very long time.

The initial injection of stimulus money had a distinctly positive impact on the economy. Unemployment trended down and much of the population had money once again to spend on goods and services. But after two years, prices of virtually everything, including food, fuel and real estate began to escalate. Official published government statistics reported inflation at a steady rate of about nine percent, but the true rate of inflation was closer to fifteen percent. Within five years prices and wages had virtually doubled.

The Subordinates in the legislature complained bitterly that the scourge of inflation had disproportionately impacted their constituents. It was true. The doubling of both prices and incomes would seem to leave everyone in the same relative financial position, but spokesmen for the Subordinates were quick to point out that the usual gap between rich and poor had also doubled. The fact that the magnitude of that gap in real — that is, non-inflated — Gildars had not changed was a detail that the Subordinates preferred to ignore. It was true, however, that the wealthiest citizens had benefited the most from the construction projects initiated by the economic stimulus.

The cost of living increases resulted in more citizens dependent on government social programs. The Subordinates had slowly added seats in the Legislature, gaining votes by promising more in the way of social welfare programs. In order to fund these programs, the banks bought billions in long term bonds from the Treasury using Gildars printed by the very same Treasury and exchanged for bank stocks. With a majority in the Legislature, the Subordinates would soon hold two of the three Administrator seats. On the day before the third Administrator seat changed hands, the outgoing and new incoming Administrators had the following exchange in front of the Legislative Assembly:

"As I prepare to leave this government, I have much concern for the future of our planet. I ask that you bring to your remembrance an earlier and more prosperous time for our people — to the years before the Grand Expedition when the Treasury coffers were full and taxes were low. Even the poorest of our citizens enjoyed a standard of living far higher than today. And now the leaders of the majority Subordinate Party are prepared to embark on an economic plan to raise taxes — a singularly bad idea that can only plunge us deeper into economic malaise."

The new incoming Administrator asked to be recognized. "I am sure that everyone here present joins with me in thanking the Honorable Administrator for her many years of service as she prepares to leave the government. But I would be remiss if I failed to point out that during her tenure, the wealthiest of our citizens — those constituents of the opposition Patrician Party — have increased their wealth so disproportionately that the gap between the rich and poor on this planet has widened substantially. At the end of her chapter in Unification Government politics, how can she justify that many citizens are relatively much poorer, much less well housed and much less provided for than before she began her role as Administrator?"

The outgoing Administrator responded, "We could do no better than to return to the policies of thirty years ago. The Honorable Representative — soon to be Honorable Administrator occupying this very seat — is saying that he would rather that the poor were poorer, provided that the rich were less rich. This is a recipe that can never increase wealth for anyone. Yet this is the policy that has always been embraced by the Subordinate Party." It was a serious charge; certainly believed by nearly every member of the conservative Patrician Party, but hardly ever voiced in polite mixed company. A hush fell over the entire assembly. The Administrator paused and looked about the room before continuing. "I now bid you farewell and wish you all the best."

As the outgoing Administrator stepped down from the podium, a handful of legislators stood and began to applaud, joined quickly by most of her fellow Patricians and several members of the Disciples Party. Every Subordinate in the hall as well as recently elected members of the new Anarchist Party remained in their seats with hands folded in their laps.

CHAPTER FIFTEEN

Yunnan Province
Five Years after the Arrival

HONGMIN AND HIS FAMILY separated from the young couple shortly after daybreak — the couple heading back to the river and Hongmin leading his family up the mountain toward their destination, the village in the Valley of Chiang-Ri. Before setting off, the young woman hugged Li-Hua, thanking her for the small package of cooked rice that would help sustain them on their journey down the mountain.

The trail leading higher from their campsite was not markedly different from what they experienced the day before. Vegetation was somewhat less abundant and although the mountain path itself was a little rockier, the travelers were still able to make good time. By late afternoon they had reached the end of the trail. Up ahead they could see the footbridge over the gorge that would lead them to their final destination.

"WHAT IS IT THAT you travelers seek?" The guard spoke in a gruff manner; his hand on the hilt of the sword at his waist. The second guard stood by with his crossbow aimed at Hongmin's chest. The children were frightened and clung to their mothers' legs.

Hongmin answered in a deferential tone, "We have traveled many suns to arrive at this place, and we seek refuge in the village of Chiang-Ri."

The first guard motioned for them to step forward and barked out an order, "Show me your hands." The adults did as they were told. "And now the children." The two mothers grasped each of the children by their forearms, raising each child's hands for the guard to inspect. When little Hui-Ying began to cry, the guard bent down on one knee, holding the little girl's hands in his own, softly stroking her fingers and palms. The second guard lowered his crossbow. "What is your name, child?"

"Hui-Ying," she answered softly.

Now in a more pleasant tone, the first guard looked up at Hongmin and asked, "Who is it that sent you here?"

"His name is Landon. He came to our village long ago, from far away." Hongmin pointed to the sky. The guard summoned a sentry at the far end of the footbridge with a wave. The sentry came quickly, crossing the bridge to where the others were waiting.

"This little girl has the required credentials for citizenship in Chiang-Ri. You will escort her and her family to the village and make certain that someone will see to their needs."

The sentry pointed at Hongmin's waistband and spoke. "You must give up your weapon. You will not need it, and no weapons are permitted in Chiang-Ri. It will be returned to you should you choose to leave the village at any time." Hongmin passed his dagger to the sentry, who then motioned for the family to follow him across the footbridge. "It is too far to fall from this bridge," he warned, "so walk slowly and hold on to the rope railing for safety." The footbridge seemed to sway a little from side to side as they passed the midpoint, but all safely reached the far end — the sentry leading, then the women with Sheng between, followed by Hongmin holding little Hui-Ying against his shoulder with one arm and grasping the rope rail with his other hand.

THEY HAD ARRIVED AT THE SUMMIT of the mountain. The floor of the gorge they crossed over was more than two hundred meters below the footbridge, and there was no other visible access to this side of the mountain unless one was adept at scaling shear rock walls. For the next hundred meters beyond the footbridge they followed a steadily descending narrow twisted path that had been cut through solid rock. The walls on each side were three to four meters high. The sentry stopped the travelers at the end of the path and exclaimed, "Welcome to the Valley of Chiang-Ri."

The view that they beheld was breathtaking: the green valley below them was surrounded by a ring of purple mountains, and a deep blue lake covered the valley floor. The village was situated at the far edge of the lake and extended up the distant slope of the valley; the terra cotta roofs illuminated brightly by the sun now low in the sky. Neat rows of crops were visible on the terraced slopes that covered the rest of the valley on either side of the village. Directly ahead of them was a stone stairway nearly two meters wide that extended a quarter-mile down to the lake.

"No, please, you must not. . . ." The sentry was pleading with Li-Hua who was crying with joy and had fallen at the sentry's feet, thanking him over and over for allowing them to enter this place. "Please, we must proceed to the village while it is still light."

Hongmin helped his wife to her feet and the family — led by their guide — made their way down the stone stairway to the lake and village that lay before them.

THE STEPS THAT LED DOWN to the valley floor ended just ten meters from the lake's edge. From there, the travelers were led along a paved walkway that ran near the edge of the water in a counter-clockwise direction around the lake. Now it was nearly dark and up ahead they could barely make out a human figure walking in their direction, stopping every few meters along the way, setting aflame one pole-mounted torch after another until a dozen were burning brightly, illuminating the walkway. The guide whispered to Hongmin that the torches were lit only for special occasions, as when the village leaders wished to welcome new arrivals.

Now they could see the human figure more clearly. He was waiting for the travelers under the light of the last torch. As they approached, all eyes were drawn to his purple robe that extended all the way to the ground. He bowed deeply and without saying a word motioned for the visitors to follow him back along the lighted path. Meanwhile, their guide turned on his heel and headed back in the direction from which they had come.

It was two steps up to a paved terrace that extended from an overhang above the edge of the water to a lighted fire pit under a high pavilion with an open roof constructed from large hewn wooden beams. The couple that had been seated on a bench facing the fire pit rose to meet the travelers.

The woman wore a colorful print that shimmered in the flickering light of the fire pit. She reached out toward the two women and grasped a hand of each with her own hands. "Welcome to Chiang-Ri," she said, smiling broadly. Her companion stood behind and to one side, his hands clasped together.

Hongmin recognized the couple and exclaimed excitedly, "You are from the ship—the vessel from the stars—that crashed near our village almost five years ago." It was the Geology Specialist from the ship and his technician assistant.

"Is that you, Hongmin? And Li-Hua? I am sorry I did not recognize you. Come closer to the light." The woman bent down in front of Hui-Ying and grasped the little girl's hands. "And who are you? What a pretty amulet you have."

"Her name is Hui-Ying. The amulet was a gift from her father, Landon. And this is her mother," said Hongmin, extending one hand toward his sister-in-law. Jia-Li bowed facing the woman.

"So tell us, Hongmin, how is it that you came to Chiang-Ri?"

"There was big trouble in our village. We were in danger and Landon sent us away. Unfortunately, I bring you bad news about some of your fellow travelers."

CHAPTER SIXTEEN

Guangling, near Beijing, 1968

IT HAD BEEN NEARLY TWO YEARS since Professor Tsum had been taken to the collective at Guangling. The instructor from the school who accompanied him had been sent home months earlier. Apparently, Lin Baio had successfully completed his "re-education curriculum" more quickly than expected as judged by the Red Guard leadership at the collective. In contrast, it was determined that Professor Tsum was likely in need of a few more months of "attitude readjustment." Over time, the Red Guard handlers began to take pride in their ability to distinguish between those who were sincere in the rededication of their lives to the ideals of Chairman Mao in contrast to those who would simply recite the responses that their handlers hoped to hear.

Many of the collective's extended-term residents held the same view as the Professor. They would avoid any open criticism of their handlers or express disagreement with the official goals of the Cultural Revolution, but internally they remained steadfast in their opposition to the State and supported the ideals of individual freedom. Their lack of expressed enthusiasm for the Revolution usually marked them as reprobates in need of further attitude adjustment.

As the second full year of his internment came to an end, the harsh schedule of labor at the collective was eased somewhat. The Red Guard personnel in charge were replaced, then replaced again after only a few weeks. Rumors began to circulate that the Communist Central Committee was concerned that the Red Guards had become far too powerful and independent and that they should be disbanded. The flow of new inductees to the collective came to a virtual halt; there were only seven individuals in the last group of arrivals. One of them was another former colleague of Professor Tsum.

"Tell me, Feng, how is it that you were able to avoid the reeducation camps for so long? Especially as I always suspected you of being a dangerous counter-revolutionary." The two men laughed heartily at the Professor's satirical remark. Feng stopped laughing briefly as he looked about to assure himself that there was no one within earshot.

"Unhappily, I avoided nothing. This is the second collective to which I have been assigned. They sent me to a camp in the North only days after you were taken from the University. The camp was shut down maybe one month ago and we were allowed to go home, but they came for me again three days ago and sent me here."

"Poor Feng. You should have kept your opinions to yourself, but that was always a difficult thing for you."

"You are correct, Tsum Nui, I guess I am just too hard-headed for my own good." They laughed again.

"Now, tell me my friend. What has become of the University in Beijing?"

"For two years, it has been all but closed down, but there are good signs: many of the staff members are returning and I have heard that classes will resume in maybe one or two months. But I bring other important news: I saw your old friend, Professor Chu. He asked about you. He was very concerned when I told him where you were. Then he asked about your wife and daughter, but I had no other information for him."

"That is some good news. It has been so long since I have heard any word about him; I thought that he was probably dead."

"In truth, he did not look well. He was recently released from prison. I told him that maybe I could get word to you. At the time, I did not think that I would be bringing you this message in person." Feng laughed again, but continued on a more serious note, "He is staying with his younger sister and her husband on Beiwa Road. Do you know the place?"

"Yes. I have been there. If I remember correctly, they live behind the small market at that location."

"Yes, that is the place. He said that it is important that he see you soon, if it was at all possible."

THE MORNING STARTED in a strange way. Every day for the past two years Professor Tsum and the others in the men's dormitory were awakened by a patrol of two or three recent Red Guard recruits, banging their batons on the metal frames of the sleeping men's cots as they marched through the building shouting appropriate Maoist slogans, warning in a not-so-gentle manner that it was time to start the day's activities. But not today. No guards had appeared and the sun was already getting high in the sky.

The residents were unsure of what they should do. They dressed and waited, sitting on their cots, for the Red Guard supervisor who came every morning to direct them to their work assignments. But no Red Guard personnel entered the building that day. Finally, a youth from the adjacent dormitory building that housed the younger men at the collective ran in and shouted, "Chairman Mao has decreed that the goals of the Cultural Revolution have been attained, and that we may all return to our homes and work." The men, mostly smiling, spoke to each other in subdued tones as they gathered their belongings and filed out of the building.

IT TOOK PROFESSOR TSUM THREE DAYS to reach the city. It would have taken longer except that the driver of a vegetable truck headed for the University offered him a ride on the third morning. He was thankful for the ride and for the meal of raw turnips and carrots he consumed on the way: the Professor hadn't eaten anything during the previous two days.

It was mid-afternoon when the driver backed up to the rear door of the kitchen at the Administration Building. Professor Tsum thanked the driver and made his way to the Anthropology Department building where his former office was located. The building was open, but deserted. The hallway leading to the faculty offices was strewn with papers. *"It will be months,"* he thought to himself, *"before this place could be returned to its former condition."*

Upon finding and entering his own office he hardly recognized the contents. His personal library of books had been knocked off their shelves. Desk drawers were pulled out with contents dumped on the floor. His desk chair was missing and papers were everywhere. He looked about the office for a few minutes, slowly shaking his head, first in disbelief and then in helpless resignation. He pulled his office door closed behind him and headed out of the building. Thirty minutes later he entered the market on Beiwa Road.

"IF YOU DON'T SEE what you want, be sure to ask," the female clerk announced. "We have chickens outside and there is fresh meat as my husband butchered a hog this morning."

"You don't remember me?"

"No, sir."

"My name is Tsum Um Nui. I taught at the University with your brother. I was told he would be here."

"Please excuse me for a moment." The woman turned to her left and walked behind the counter for several paces, then up two stairs, pushing aside the hanging beads in the doorway that separated the market from the proprietor's living quarters at the rear of the building. A minute later, Professor Chu descended the two stairs, steadying himself with a cane. He had a weak smile on his face as he greeted Professor Tsum.

CHAPTER SEVENTEEN

Alexandria Virginia
Present Day

"SO FOR SEVERAL YEARS you heard nothing from Professor Chu—not until your colleague Feng came to the collective?" Amanda picked up the voice recorder from the coffee table to verify that it was still recording.

"Yes, that is correct. On the day that I met with him at the home of his sister, we were together for the rest of afternoon and all the next day. It was good that we had that time together, for I had many questions."

"What questions?"

"I understood why I was marked for re-education by the Red Guards. I was known at University for being a free thinker. Many suspected—but could not prove—that I supported the Kuomintang during the Revolution, but did not support either side. Any of my students can confirm that my class lectures often emphasized positive aspects of Western culture and politics. All these things explain why I was sent to the collective for two years. But why was Professor Chu subjected to a harsh prison sentence when he committed no crimes against the State? I asked him this question because he never spoke out against the regime or promoted counter-revolutionary ideas at the University."

"What was the Professor's explanation?"

"First of all, Professor Chu was considered to be a member of the privileged class before the Revolution. His family members were landowners and he had great personal wealth. But the findings of his 1938 expedition to Bayan Har suggested that thousands of years of Chinese culture and progress had extra-terrestrial roots—a concept that was incompatible with Maoist thought.

"All of these facts were brought up during Professor Chu's interrogation and subsequent trial. He was forced to recant the findings of the expedition; that it was all part of an elaborate hoax intended to bring him academic fame and fortune. He told me that during his interrogation he was questioned about his association from years earlier with a famous English writer. His name was James Hilton."

"James Hilton? I'm familiar with his work," declared Roger. "Hilton wrote a couple of best-selling novels—*Goodbye, Mr. Chips* and *Lost Horizon*. I believe both were made into popular movies. What was the connection between Professor Chu and James Hilton?"

Tsum Um Nui continued, "Professor Chu told me—"

"Father?" The interrogative from Melanie Tsum interrupted the Professor.

"What is it, child?"

"Do we need to get into this part of the story—now?"

"What is the difference, child? Now or later? There is no reason for you to be embarrassed." Roger and Amanda looked at each other quizzically, not knowing where this conversation was going. Melanie folded her arms in front of her and looked down as Professor Tsum continued from where he had left off. "Professor Chu told me that Mister Hilton had come to Chu's office at the University in Chengdu. It was a few months after a summary of the 1938 expedition had been published in local newspaper and received some international attention—popular attention, not academic. Hilton was in Peking at the time and an associate showed the article to him. What intrigued Mister Hilton—and then induced him to seek out Professor Chu—was the startling account of the expedition's discovery of bone fragments—bones from hands and feet with only four phalanges.

"It seems that when Mister Hilton was doing research for his novel years earlier, he travel through much of Sichuan and Yunnan Provinces near border with Tibet. He told Professor Chu that he had visited a remote village where many of the women—maybe one-third of village women—had the same physical trait: three fingers and a thumb on each hand and just four toes on each foot.

"Now at this point, Professor Chu was also much interested. The village that Hilton visited was about 400 kilometers from Chengdu and the Professor was determined to make the trip. Hilton was able to mark the approximate location on a map, but explained that access to village was difficult. It was in a valley surrounded by high mountains— very isolated—and the only access was narrow footpath that generations of goat herders had managed to carve out of the face of mountain."

"So tell us, did the Professor reach the village?" The question from Roger brought a smile to Amanda's face. It was as if they were seated around a campfire and Professor Tsum was narrating a ghost story.

"Yes. Professor Chu found village. It took him ten days, but he found it. And he stayed there for several years."

"Did he tell you the name of the village? Maybe we can find it on a map."

"Professor Chu asked many of the residents, but most just called it *Twen*—which simply means *village*. It was not until he met with a few of the village old people who confirmed that there was once an ancient name for the village. They called it *Chiang-Ri*. They also told the Professor that long before the footpath was carved in the mountain, the only access to village was a footbridge across a gorge between two mountains. The footbridge long ago disappeared.

"And the hands and feet of the women there; was it true? What James Hilton had said?"

"Yes. Many of the women exhibited this oddity."

"Only the women?" asked Amanda. She thought the claim was rather odd, but before the Professor could answer, Melanie suddenly lowered her folded arms and using the thumb and forefinger of her gloved right hand, jerked the white cotton glove from her left. She held out her bare hand and tossed the glove on the marble table top where it landed with a plop.

Melanie shouted, "Yes, only the women were cursed with this deformity!" She rose from her chair and stepped quickly away, the heels of her shoes clattering on the parquet floor and echoing from the far walls of the large room. Professor Tsum briefly raised one hand to his forehead, then lowered it to his side. He was clearly disturbed by his daughter's reaction.

"Maybe now was not the right time. She has always been sensitive about her hands and feet. No open-toed shoes." The Professor picked up the glove from the table and turned it inside out, revealing a prosthetic pinkie finger—possibly made of silicone rubber—that included an extension at the base intended to fit along the side of his daughter's hand. "And always—the white gloves. All the time in school and growing up, she tired of people staring and whispering."

"Your daughter is a beautiful woman," remarked Roger, "and nothing can take away from that."

"We wondered about the white gloves," offered Amanda, "but I can certainly understand."

"Thank you. I'm sure that Melanie would appreciate the sentiment."

"I don't mean to be disrespectful, Professor, but were you able to learn what might account for Melanie's—" Amanda paused before continuing, " —for her condition? Genetics, or something else?"

"My wife has been gone for many years. Before she retired, she was a medical researcher at the University. She was able to study data from birth records from some major cities in the eastern provinces and compare with records in the west. Naturally, there were no records available from births on farms and smaller villages. In the east, maybe one infant in two million had the same distinguishing feature. But in Sichuan and Yunnan Province, it was observed maybe once in ten thousand births, with higher frequency in some specific locations. Almost all the babies born with this condition were females."

"Was there any explanation?"

"There are two or three genetic markers involved. It is very complicated, but the simple explanation is that the condition is usually dominant in females, but recessive in males. That means that a male child born from a father with even the most complete sequence of markers will not have the condition unless the mother has the trait. But a female child will often have the condition with either parent having a complete sequence of markers or both having a partial sequence."

"So it could be either you or Melanie's mother — or both — that might account for Melanie's condition."

"There is something else you should know about my daughter." But before he could explain further, the phone on the wall behind the bar ten feet from them began to ring softly. Professor Tsum hoped that his daughter would answer the extension in her bedroom, but when she did not, he rose to answer it himself.

"Yes. Can I help you?"

"Is this Professor Tsum?"

"Yes." Initially in English, the man on the phone now spoke in Mandarin.

"Listen carefully, Professor. If you care about the lives of your daughter and your new American friends, you will remain calm and pretend that I am an old friend from Chengdu. Do you understand?"

The Professor consented to the caller's demand. "Yes. It is good to hear from you after all these years."

"Very good, Professor. After we end this conversation, you will excuse yourself and come to the hotel lobby. I will be waiting for you outside the main entrance to the hotel. Come alone."

"I understand. I can do that. Goodbye."

After hanging up the phone, Professor Tsum tried to clear his mind. For a few seconds, he was unsure of what he should do, but he quickly made a decision. He wrote a note on the pad next to the phone and handed it to Roger.

"I must go to the lobby. Would you please give the message to my daughter when she comes out of her room? It is about the Dropa disc, from Bangkok."

"Certainly, Professor. Would you like me to accompany you downstairs?"

"No, it is not necessary. I do not need assistance, and I will return soon."

WHEN MELANIE TSUM EMERGED from her bedroom twenty minutes later Roger Atwood was in the kitchen area poking around in the cabinets in search of some creamer. He had made a pot of coffee. Melanie retrieved her glove from the marble top of the coffee table and pulled it on to her left hand, taking care to adjust the prosthetic pinkie. She turned and looked about before she directed her attention to Amanda, still seated near the coffee table.

"Where's my father?"

Roger was headed back toward the two women, cup in one hand and the note from Professor Tsum in the other.

"He went to the lobby after speaking with someone on the phone. I think it had something to do with the Dropa disc. He told me to give you this note." Melanie took the folded paper from Roger's hand and read it to herself.

JOHN WU
WU TAI ENGINEERING
FALLS CHURCH

"Did he tell you he was meeting this man—John Wu—in the lobby?"

"He didn't mention any names." Melanie sprinted toward the door of the suite. Roger quickly set down his coffee cup and followed her out to a nearby bank of elevators. When Roger caught up with her, he was apologetic.

"I offered to accompany him; I guess I should have insisted." When the elevator door opened at the lobby level, they looked about but there was no sign of the Professor. The clerk at the front desk was no help and referred them to the concierge at the front door.

"Have you seen an elderly Asian man in the last few minutes?"

"Maybe ten minutes ago. I held the door for him."

"Did you happen to see where he went?"

"There was a younger man waiting out here for him. They both got into the back seat of a black Lincoln and drove away."

Melanie Tsum was very upset. "I need you to call the police. I believe my father was abducted."

The concierge tried to reassure her. "Your father didn't seem to be in distress, and he was not forced into that vehicle, but I'll make the call if you wish."

"Yes, please."

The concierge waited for the 911 Operator to answer. "That is correct, ma'am, the Ferndale Hotel. We have a guest here who believes her father was kidnapped." Pause. "Let me have you speak with her directly." He handed the phone to Melanie. By now Amanda had come from the suite and joined the group gathered about the concierge desk.

Melanie looked about as she waited for the operator's first question. "Melanie — Melanie Tsum. T-S-U-M." Pause. "My father, same last name. He was seen getting into a stranger's car twenty minutes ago." Pause. "Yes, he is quite elderly." Pause. "Thank you." She handed the phone back to the concierge. "They're sending someone."

THE INVESTIGATING OFFICERS first questioned the concierge, then Melanie. When she told them about the suite being ransacked two days earlier, one of the officers spoke with the hotel manager and asked if a police report had been filed. *No, the police had not been called,* he was embarrassed to admit. The officer understood why: Reports of persons unknown breaking into guest rooms tended to undermine public confidence in the establishment, something that management tried to avoid. What the officer failed to understand was why the hotel management chose to ignore the broken video camera that could have captured the entire incident. It had been inoperable for weeks.

After completing their investigation at the hotel, the officers met with Melanie. Until now, they had gathered little information that might lead to the return of her father. They would track down John Wu to see if he was involved in the abduction or maybe knew something that might move the investigation forward. The officers promised to keep Melanie informed and reminded her that the Professor might just return to the hotel on his own.

CHAPTER EIGHTEEN

Tiwanaku, Bolivia
Three years after the Arrival

WHEN FRANCISCO PIZARRO arrived on the coast of what is now modern-day Ecuador with his band of soldiers in 1532, he encountered a surprisingly advanced society. Historians agree that the Inca represented the greatest Pre-Columbian civilization in the western world. The Inca Empire extended from Tiwanaku in Bolivia and south into Chile—more than one million square kilometers in all. The factors responsible for the creation of such an advanced culture are the subject of much present-day debate.

The Inca had accumulated enormous wealth and power in a relatively short time. Experts generally agree that expansion began about the middle of the 13th century as Inca influence spread from the capital of Cusco in Peru to the surrounding country.

As with many of his sixteenth century contemporaries, Pizarro was a Conquistador—a romantic title for a soldier of fortune whose desire to enrich himself far exceeded the often stated lofty purpose of bringing the Word of God to the heathen hordes.

It is virtually unimaginable that Pizarro and his band of two hundred soldiers were able to bring down such a great and powerful nation. But it was the arrogance of Atahualpa — the sovereign emperor of the Inca — that made it all possible by underestimating both Pizarro's tactical ability and his willingness to engage in treachery to accomplish his goals. Three rooms full of gold and silver were offered and accepted as ransom for release of the captured Inca leader who was subsequently subjected to the sham of a trial and executed by his captors. Spanish ships carried the ransom treasure back to Pizarro's homeland to be divided among the Conquistador, his partners in conquest and the Crown.

The Inca Empire had its roots in Tiwanaku. Although never reaching the level or breadth of the Inca Empire, Tiwanaku was impressive in its own right. It was an agrarian civilization with its political center at the city of the same name on the southern shore of Lake Titicaca at 3,800 meters elevation. Experts claim that Tiwanaku was the undisputed power in the region for the preceding 500 years; or maybe — according to some — for much, much longer.

It is unfortunate that precious little is known about the ancestors of the Tiwanaku people. Contributing to this lack of knowledge is the fact that neither the Tiwanaku nation nor their Inca descendants possessed a written language. Estimates of the age of the earliest civilization vary widely.

Most conservative estimates place the origins of Tiwanaku at about 1,500 BC—some 3,600 years old. However, a twentieth-century researcher, Arthur Posnansky, claimed that Tiwanaku had its beginnings 17,000 years ago and was the point of origin of the Mayans—as well as the Inca—and virtually every other Western civilization. Posnansky's dating was based on the cyclic precession of the tilt of the earth's axis—a 41,000 year cycle. His measurements of the astronomical alignment at the Temple of Kalasasaya at Tiwanaku Site place the age of the Temple at the point in the cycle dating back 17,000 years.

Although many contemporary archaeologists dispute this age estimate, Posnansky's methodology is logically sound and his alignment measurements have been confirmed. There are, however, some important assumptions on which this age estimate is based. Possible sources of error in Posnansky's work include the following: (1) It is not known if the regular 41,000 year precession cycle is indeed an accurate model of variation in the earth's axial tilt, (2) the original builders of the Temple may not have been exactly precise in replicating the then current astronomical alignment during construction and (3) an earthquake or other cataclysmic event of sufficient magnitude may have occurred after construction that could affect the original builder's alignment.

The true age of Tiwanaku most likely lies somewhere between the extreme age values cited above. Someday it may be shown that the origin coincides closely with the arrival of eight travelers from a distant planet circling a non-descript star near a region of the celestial sphere known to some as the *Beak of the Turtle*.

THE ARRIVAL OF THE SCOUT SHIP to the environs of Tiwanaku was immediately welcomed as a positive event by the local population. Although first choosing to observe from a respectful distance, few locals seemed to express fear or even concern; those emotions apparently no match for their curiosity. When the first travelers emerged from their craft, they were immediately greeted with smiles and friendly shouts.

After successful verbal communication was established, the locals reluctantly accepted the visitors' emphatic assurance that they were not gods, but no amount of persuasion could convince them that the friendly strangers—exhibiting such wondrous knowledge and powers—were not at least *sent* by one of the gods. It became a consensus of the locals that the travelers were sent to them by Viracocha, perhaps their most important god, creator of all things including the sun, moon, stars and even time.

Before the arrival of the visitors, the inhabitants of the four or five villages in the surrounding area lived peacefully with one another, but life was often a struggle. The fortunes of the locals depended each year on weather conditions. Drought was the frequent cause of crop failure and starvation for many. The high altitude all but guaranteed a short growing season and low crop yields due to freezing temperatures. Consequently, potatoes became a staple of their diet as the inclement weather had less impact on the crops of potatoes and other tubers. Highly prized by the most successful farmers were their small herds of llama and alpaca, also dependent upon the weather for the necessary abundance of local grasses.

The Agriculture Specialist from the crew and her male assistant spent much of the first winter reviewing the methods of the local farmers. Before the next planting season they had created test plots that promised improved yields and would mitigate effects of both drought and cold weather conditions. A local lime deposit provided a source of raw material to create a primitive gunite lining for a water reservoir and ponds that could be used for raising fish. Many of the local men provided the labor needed to complete these projects.

Perhaps their most important innovation was the construction of shallow canals between the raised rows of crops. The water-filled canals supplied the necessary moisture for growth, but also served to extend the growing season by absorbing heat from solar radiation during daylight hours and releasing it at night, preventing frost damage from any early cold snap before crops were fully mature.

The locals were quick to adopt the new methods. By the third year, crop yields had more than doubled on the original acreage and more land was brought under cultivation. The herds of llama and alpaca grew larger and healthier. Encouraged by prospects for their future, the villagers happily welcomed the bumper crop of new babies. The Medical Officer from the ship held frequent courses in midwifery with the arrival of each new birth event. The older women from the villages understood the importance of passing on what they had learned from the Medical Officer, so that long after the Visitors had departed, untold numbers of mothers and infants would now more easily survive the ordeal of child bearing.

The Mission Commander aboard the mother ship was pleased to receive the positive reports from the members of the first scout ship team. With one crew of eight long since lost and presumed dead and another reporting problems from hostile locals, the reports of the successes achieved in Tiwanaku were welcome indeed.

CHAPTER NINETEEN

Bayan Har Mountains, China
18 Months after the Arrival

LANDON HAD POLITELY DECLINED two previous invitations from his friend to come to his home for the stated purpose of sharing a meal together. Both he and Hongmin understood that the real purpose was for Landon and Hongmin's Sister-in-Law, Jia-Li, to meet and see if there was any common interest between them—that is, any mutual interest in establishing a personal relationship.

"Welcome to my home, Landon. You have met my wife, Li-Hua." The woman smiled and bowed politely—not a deep bow—with her hands in front of her, clasped together. "And this is our son, Sheng." Hongmin held the boy in front of him, grasping both shoulders. Sheng was five years old.

"Yes, we have met before. It is good to see you again, and thank you for inviting me to your home," replied Landon. They were in the largest of three rooms in the simple rock structure. The ceiling sloped down in the direction of the two smaller rooms with the underside of roof shingles visible, attached to several log beams. There were two window openings in opposing rock walls, adjacent to the wall that included the front door. The shutters opened outward and when fully opened they rested against the outside walls of the structure. There were no doors on either of the two smaller rooms — probably sleeping quarters.

"And this young woman . . ." Hongmin gestured toward his Sister-in-Law. ". . . is the sister of my wife. Her name is Jia-Li." As Landon took a few steps toward the young woman, she extended her right hand slowly until Landon offered his. She grasped his hand lightly and made a slight bow in his direction. Jia-Li was dressed in a medium-brown colored wrap that fell below her calf. She wore an orange scarf at her neck, under the wrap that was cinched at the waist with a matching orange fabric tie.

"I am happy that we had this chance to meet, Jia-Li." The woman smiled politely for a moment, then lowered her eyes, offering a second shallow bow.

Hongmin beckoned for his family and guest to seat themselves on the floor around the low rectangular table near the center of the room. Five carved wooden plates marked the seating locations. Hongmin stepped outside to an outdoor stone grill and returned with several cuts of broiled rabbit on a flat board that he placed at the center of the table. Li-Hua had prepared two wooden bowls of vegetables, one containing cooked cabbage and a second full of spindly raw carrots.

Hongmin sat at the head of the table with his wife and son along one side, opposite Landon and Jia-Li who were seated next to each other. They ate with chop sticks and the adults drank huangjju — a dark yellow wine made from fermented rice and millet.

The topics of dinner conversation varied widely. Landon asked Hongmin about the year's grain crop. *It will be a good harvest if the rain continues through the growing season.* Li-Hua had heard about the couple from the ship who had traveled to the distant mountain village. Had they returned safely? *Yes.* What was the village like? *It was built near a lake, with well-designed stone buildings with tile roofs.* Sheng asked if Landon had been able to hear from his fellow travelers in the sky using the "talking wires" device that his father had helped Landon build. *No, not yet.*

When the meal was over Li-Hua suggested that the couple might want to take a walk. "It is a very beautiful evening, you should go," she said. It was beginning to get dark and Li-Hua lit an oil lamp.

Sheng immediately jumped up and exclaimed, "I want to go for a walk! Can I go?"

"No," replied Hongmin. "It is your bed time." Sheng looked down, dejected.

"They can I go to bed a little later? I will help mama clear the table."

"Very well," replied Hongmin.

THE COUPLE STEPPED OUT OF THE HOUSE and down the well-traveled path past Hongmin's neighbors. Kai, the name Landon had given his mixed shepherd breed dog, joined them on the path. The animal had come with Landon to Hongmin's house and had been waiting for his master outside the door. The path ended at the crest of a hill overlooking a narrow canyon. The full moon was very bright behind some wisps of clouds, just above the horizon to the east. It really was a beautiful evening.

"Do you have such a beautiful moon as this in the place from where you came?"

"We have two moons," replied Landon, "but neither is so large or beautiful as this one. I can show you where my home is. Would you like to see?"

"Yes."

Landon moved behind Jia-Li, resting his hands lightly on her shoulders and guided her body gently to the right so that they were facing southwest. He then extended his right arm over her shoulder, pointing to the night sky.

"You see the three bright stars near where I am pointing?"

"Yes, I see them."

"My home is a place like this planet, in the direction between those three stars."

"I see some fainter lights there. Is one of those your home?"

"No, my home planet and the star that is our sun are much too far away to see from this place."

"And so you will return to your home someday soon?"

Landon hesitated before answering. "Someday, yes, I hope to return there. But it will not be soon. Our Commander tells me that we will likely remain in this place for at least three more years, or until we are no longer welcome. And if we are unable to contact our friends to come and find us, we may never leave this place."

"I hope that you can stay here a very long time."

Landon stepped from behind Jia-Li to face her, drawing her close to his body and put his arms around her. "I hope so, too."

They sat for a long time, watching as the moon rose above the low lying clouds. Landon didn't know if it would impolite to ask Jia-Li about her husband and marriage, but he was curious.

"It must have been a very difficult time for you when you lost your husband. Hongmin told me about it."

"What did he tell you?"

"Not very much. He said that your husband was hunting when he fell from the side of the mountain and died from his injuries."

"Yes, it is true. We were together for two years. At first we were very happy, but after a few months, my husband changed. He spent much time away from home. He became close friends with the son of the village chief and they would often go away together on hunting trips. It was then that he began to treat me poorly. He often beat me and told me that

I was useless for I did not bear him children. After a time I found myself to be happy only when he was away from home and could not hurt me. When I heard that he had died, I was not sad. I felt only relief." Landon reached over and grasped Jia-Li's hand in his own.

"I am sorry that you had such an unhappy marriage."

"After my husband died, my sister and Hongmin were kind enough to take me into their home. So it has been much better for me since then. Some of my husband's old friends have come to see me, but I was not interested in another man—not until now." She smiled at Landon.

They sat without speaking for a time, each in thought, separately considering the intimacy of the moment they had shared. But now it was late, and Jia-Li spoke, "We should return to the house now. My sister will be worried." Landon agreed. As they rose to leave, Jia-Li added, "Tell me, Landon, what else did Hongmin say about me?"

"He said you were very beautiful, and he was right."

CHAPTER TWENTY

State of Delaware
Present Day

THE FOUR ASIAN MEN who had spirited Professor Tsum from the Ferndale Hotel in Alexandria had taken him to a safe house just outside Smyrna, Delaware. They arrived in the late afternoon and stayed overnight. Early the next morning they exchanged the Town Car for a late model Dodge van at the safe house and headed north on Delaware State Highway One.

"I ask you again, what is it you want with me?" Professor Tsum was seated in the rear between two of the Asians and spoke in his Sichuan dialect. The man in charge sat in the front passenger seat and turned his head to reply to the professor.

"Please, Professor Tsum, remember that we are in America. Let us speak English." His tone was sarcastic.

"Very well, but can you answer me?"

"We want nothing *from* you, Professor — we want you. Or to be more precise, it is the government of the country you abandoned years ago that wants you. You have been missed."

Within forty-five minutes they arrived at the main gate at the Port of Wilmington. The driver handed his photo ID and a wharf pass to the guard at the gate and they were cleared to enter. A crane near the middle of the wharf was loading the hold of the Chinese flag vessel *Tian Zhou* with lumber from flat cars on a nearby railroad siding. The ship was on the small side for a cargo vessel with an overall length of just 64 meters, 470 gross tons.

The leader of the gang of four exited the parked vehicle and ascended the gangplank. The Professor and the others in the van watched as the leader conversed with a uniformed crew member on the deck of the *Tian Zhou* near the bridge. After several minutes, the leader returned to the vehicle.

"Come, Professor. This ship leaves port in three days. You will be confined to your cabin, but it should be a pleasant voyage. When it docks in Caracas, you will be escorted to the airport for a flight to Beijing."

THE POLICE DETECTIVE ASSIGNED to the case of Professor Tsum's disappearance had come to Melanie's hotel in Alexandria.

"I hope you have brought me some good news regarding my father, Detective."

"Not exactly, Ms Tsum, but we have added more people to the case, and the State Police have been brought in. One of their officers suggested that it might have been a kidnapping for ransom. I'm sure you would have called, but I'm here to see if anyone has attempted to contact you."

"No. No one."

"Well, I will get in touch with you immediately if anything breaks."

"Thank you, Detective."

"And you should know that we interviewed John Wu. He told us that he knew your father when they were both at the University in Beijing—before Doctor Wu emigrated to the U.S. Apparently Wu had done some engineering work related to one of your father's research projects and they kept in contact through the years. He was surprised to hear of the abduction. We're pretty sure he has no involvement. Wu learned from an email that your father was coming to Virginia and that he should expect some parcel. Maybe it will provide a clue that will lead to your father's return."

"We can only hope."

CHAPTER TWENTY-ONE

The Jordan Valley
3 Months after the Arrival

T HE EFFORTS OF THE CREW from the second scout ship to engage the local population in the Jordan Valley had proved frustrating indeed. The encounter outside the gate of the walled city was so far the only openly hostile encounter with the locals, but — with one exception — every other individual or small group they happened upon seemed stubbornly fearful, suspicious or indifferent. Marlot was the exception, and the coincidence that he admitted to being a stranger himself had escaped no one's attention.

In the weeks following their first meeting, Marlot had come to the scout ship on multiple occasions. Usually he came alone, but sometimes with his two teenage daughters in tow. His wife accompanied them only once. Marlot later explained that his wife had a penchant for life in the city — the market place, social activities and gossiping with her friends and neighbors. There was little that interested her outside the city walls. In contrast, Marlot had little use for the city and the surrounding region. "I wish we had never come to this land," he lamented.

Marlot had brought a shoulder of lamb to share with several members of the crew. He had prepared it over an open fire, and now that the meal was over, they all sat around the fire. The evening was cool and the warmth from the fire felt good.

"How is it that you and your family decided to settle here?" The Commander of the scout ship asked the question that was on the minds of many of his crew members as well.

"It is a long story. I will start from the beginning, if you care to hear it."

"Yes, tell us."

"When I was much younger, I lived in a place called Ur—a land a great distance from here—in the East. My ancestors had lived there for many generations after the Great Flood. After my father died, my grandfather and my uncle decided that we must move away. So my uncle with his wife and my grandfather and I travel to a place called Haran. My grandfather was old and died in that place, and then my uncle announces that we are to travel further west—that he has been told to leave Haran."

"Told to leave? Told by whom?"

"My uncle received a vision from the Lord God." This statement from Marlot received a mixed response from the crew. Three of the crew members were Believers; five were not.

"So you are a Believer?" The question came from the Commander.

"If you are asking if I believe in the one true God, then yes, I do."

One of the non-Believers in the crew asked, "Did you also receive this vision from your god?"

"No, it was my uncle's vision."

"Have you ever received any sort of vision from your god?"

The Commander interrupted before Marlot could reply. "Can we not hear the rest of the story from Marlot, before we start debating among ourselves over the existence of God? Marlot, you were about to tell us about leaving Haran with your uncle."

"Yes. Understand that when I talk about moving from place to place, that it was not simply a matter of packing a few things on a donkey and setting off in one direction or another. My people are herdsmen. My uncle and I own large flocks of sheep and many cattle, all tended by extended family members and helpers and their families. We had to pitch our tents where there would be adequate water and grazing for the animals, sometimes staying at one location for weeks waiting for the men we sent ahead to return and tell us where our next place to stop and rest would be. It had taken nearly a year to move from Ur to Haran, and so to move to a new place was not a decision taken lightly."

"Your uncle was the patriarch of the family, so everyone would naturally agree to his decision. Correct?"

"Yes, all were in agreement; especially after learning of the vision from the Lord God. But it was a difficult time for us. After traveling a great distance and finding famine in the land, we continued on to Egypt. It was not the destination we were promised, but we prospered there and stayed for several seasons."

"Where is this place, that you call 'Egypt'?"

"It is in the West. We traveled along the shore of the Great Sea for many weeks, until we reached the wide river that flows north into the sea."

"There was no famine in Egypt?"

"No. There is rich farmland where the river meets the sea. Each year — after the river rises high — the land is renewed and so the ground is always fertile. Our herds grew in size and we added much wealth to our families."

"Why then did you leave Egypt?"

"Yes," remarked another crew member, "why would you leave if you had become so prosperous there?"

"There are many reasons. Most important, it was not the land that was promised to us. And the native people in the land did not believe in the one true God. They had many gods that they worshipped — all false gods — including their sun god, Ra, and Isis, the mother goddess. If we stayed, we would eventually lose our identity and maybe our people would stop serving the Lord. Besides, we received word from the east that the drought and famine had passed."

"From what you say, it seems you had good reasons to leave, even if Egypt was good to your people."

"But there was another reason. There was a problem between my uncle and the Pharaoh regarding my uncle's wife."

"Who is the Pharaoh, and why was he important."

"Pharaoh is the king—and a god in the eyes of his people. According to their beliefs, Pharaoh was an intermediary—communicating the will of their chief gods to the people."

"So what was the problem about your uncle's wife?"

"When we arrived in Egypt, my uncle was afraid that Pharaoh would kill him and take his wife—her name was Sarai—into the palace for himself, so Pharaoh was told that Sarai was my uncle's sister, not his wife. After a season, Pharaoh did indeed take Sarai into his palace. Before long, plagues and other evils began to fall upon Pharaoh and his people.

"When Pharaoh learned the truth he was very angry and told us to immediately leave his land with all our people and livestock. And so we did. We traveled back to the East, away from the land of Egypt, and I separated myself from my uncle. I came here to the Plain of Jordan and my uncle settled with his people near Hebron."

JUST AS MARLOT was finishing his story, an aide to the Scout Ship Commander approached and whispered in the Commander's ear. "I'm sorry to interrupt, sir, but we have a serious situation: Two of our crew members on sentry duty—Fassel and Garnor—were set upon by a mob from the walled city and taken prisoner. We believe they were taken back to the city. Shall I assemble the crew?"

The Commander rose quickly. "Have our Weapons Specialists meet me here immediately. Make sure they are fully armed. If we leave soon, we can reach the walled city before dark."

Marlot expressed concern, "May I join you? Perhaps I can help get your people released. I can speak to the City Elder."

"Yes. You are welcome to come with us, but understand that there may be trouble—including violence. We intend to do what is necessary to have our crew members released."

CHAPTER TWENTY-TWO

Bayan Har Mountains, China
18 Months after the Arrival

HONGMIN CAME CALLING on the Visitor ship just one day after the dinner at Hongmin's home where Landon was introduced to Jia-Li. The COM Officer was seated at a table under the gazebo—a table piled high with electronic modules and components that he had removed from the ship.

"Hello, Landon. I see that you are still working on your talking wires. Are you making progress?" Hongmin wanted to ask Landon about last night and Jia-Li but decided it would be best not to pose that question until later.

"Maybe some time today it will be ready to test." Landon had disassembled several of the modules, removing and examining each circuit board in search of a suitable power supply as well as a crystal oscillator circuit that could send coded pulses to the dipole antenna and act as a primitive transmitter. He had succeeded in putting together a receiver of sorts using an LC filter and a two stage transistor amplifier. The output of the amplifier was wired to the audio circuit of a spare communicator. The pair of wires coiled up on the ground beside him were connected to the two legs of the dipole antenna that Hongmin had previously helped him assemble, waiting to be connected to his receiver and transmitter circuits.

"It looks very complicated. Do you think it will work?"

"It has been many years since I studied components at this level. As the ship's Communications Officer, when I found that something had failed, we would simply remove the bad module — one of the metal boxes you see here — and replace it with a new one. Not very complicated." After a few minutes, Landon set aside the circuit board he had been examining and turned toward Hongmin. "So tell me, Hongmin, did you speak with Jia-Li after I left your home last evening?"

"Yes," replied Hongmin. He was pleased that he was not the first to bring up the subject.

"And did she have anything to say about me?"

"Yes." Hongmin was being coy.

"Well, t-tell me," stammered Landon. "What did she say?"

Hongmin laughed. "She said that she likes you, and that she hoped you would come to see her again very soon. My wife and Jia-Li insisted that I come here today to find out what you think about her."

"You can tell her that I feel the same way and cannot wait until we can be together again." Landon had a broad smile on his face. "Now, hand me that coil of wire on the ground so that I can finish putting this piece of junk together."

THE EXPEDITION MOTHER SHIP, in low earth orbit some 150 kilometers above the surface, was the only source of radio transmissions that Landon's crude apparatus could potentially intercept. The two sister scout ships were far too distant. Even communication between them had to use the mother ship as a relay station. The mother ship maintained a near-equatorial orbit and so Landon reasoned that there would be ample opportunity for reception and transmission; maybe several minutes during every ninety minute orbital period during which the mother ship would be favorably positioned in the sky.

As evening twilight set in, Landon connected the power supply to a power cable from the ship's battery bank and they waited, looking to the east for the bright star-like object to poke above the horizon. Hongmin was the first to see it.

Landon switched on his receiver and began to manually sweep through the frequency band by slowly turning the adjustment knob on the LC filter. The small speaker in the disassembled communicator hissed—just static. Landon hoped to intercept any transmission from the mother ship destined for the second scout ship in the Jordan

Valley. That could not occur until the mother ship had progressed further west. It would take a few minutes for it to pass the zenith above Landon's location and begin to descend toward the western horizon, correctly positioned for radio communication with the second scout ship.

Finally, they could hear something—a spoken voice. It could only be coming from the mother ship. Landon quickly activated the transmitter. He was able to control the burst of pulses sent to the antenna using an improvised contact switch and pounded out a military distress call in code, repeating it again and again until . . . disaster! The transmitter circuit began to smoke and then caught fire. Capacitors cooked off with a loud pop. He yelled out to Hongmin, "Disconnect the power cable. Now!"

IT WAS MORNING BEFORE LANDON was able to muster sufficient courage to survey the damage to his improvised radio set. The receiver section and communicator were largely intact as was the dipole antenna. But the power supply and transmitter circuits were totally destroyed by the fire, if not by the current surge that preceded it. Finding another power supply from his collection of spare parts would not be a problem, so he guessed it would take only a few hours to get his system up and running for receiving communications. Unfortunately, there was no way to restore the ability to transmit. There were simply no more suitable parts that he could press into service.

With any luck, the mother ship received his distress signal from the night before. But in fact, there was no assurance that it even reached the mother ship; he had no means to test the strength of the signal generated by his makeshift transmitter before it failed.

After Landon restored the operation of his radio receiver, he and the other crew members listened intently to the infrequent communications from the mother ship for any sign that his brief distress signal had been received. They were able to monitor one-side of the conversations between the mother ship and scout ship personnel in what they believed to be the Jordan Valley, but there was never a mention of their own ship, or personnel or their mission. It was obvious that the Mission Commander aboard the mother ship continued to believe that they had all perished in the descent to the surface more than eighteen months earlier.

THE STARK REALIZATION that their prospects for ever returning to their home planet would remain slim had a profound impact on the attitudes and actions of both the crew members and the local population. The Geology Specialist and his technician assistant announced that they had become a couple and made a special request of the Scout Ship Commander. They asked that they be relieved of their mission responsibilities so that they could return to the distant village on the lake — the village in the Valley of Chiang-Ri — to live out their lives among the local population there. Landon began spending virtually all of his off-duty hours with Jia-Li. They were very happy together and had grown close.

But the news from the village at Bayan Har was not good. Zhang Zhu had become Chief with the recent passing of his father and was stirring up discontent among the villagers with the help of his thug minions. *"The Visitors will never leave this place,"* it was claimed, *"and before long they will make slaves of us all."*

CHAPTER TWENTY-THREE

Arlington, Virginia
Present Day

"IS THERE ANYTHING we can do to help, Roger?" It had been four days since Professor Tsum had been abducted and they hadn't heard any news from his daughter, Melanie, since the day before yesterday.

"I don't know. I feel really bad for Melanie and her father. Hopefully, the authorities can find the poor man—unharmed. So far, the professor's story is a good one. I want us to be able to tell it with a happy ending."

"I'm going to call her."

MELANIE ASKED IF THEY could come to her hotel suite that very afternoon. When Roger and Amanda arrived, they found their host understandably still very upset over the disappearance of her father.

"I am really worried. The local police have not been very helpful. They say that the case has their highest priority and they have followed up a few leads, but without results. They keep asking if I've received a ransom demand." Frustrated, she pulled the white gloves from her hands and threw them on the sofa, burying her face in her bare hands.

"What about the FBI?" Amanda asked. "Can't they help?"

"My understanding is that the FBI won't get involved unless there is evidence that the victim has been transported across state lines," offered Roger.

"What about that Federal agent at the airport? What was his name?"

"Bancroft."

"Yes, David Bancroft. He was with the U.S. Attorney's Office. Aren't they connected with the FBI somehow? He seemed fairly sympathetic about your father's case. Maybe he could help, or at least give us some advice. Didn't he give you one of his cards, Melanie?"

"Yes, he did. It must be in my purse." Melanie excused herself and retreated to her bedroom to find the business card and place a call to David Bancroft. Roger and Amanda sat on the sofa and waited.

"I have a bad feeling about this, Roger. I wouldn't want to further upset Melanie, but if the people who took Professor Tsum didn't intend to harm him, don't you think we would have heard something from someone by now?"

"Not necessarily. What if they were more interested in the Professor himself, rather than that Dropa Disc? Clearly, he is the expert on the subject— probably knows more about translating those inscriptions than any person living. Maybe there are researchers in the Chinese government in possession of the two missing discs that the Professor told us about and they want the Professor to translate the inscriptions on them."

"C'mon Roger. Pardon the mixed metaphor, but you're creating a script out of whole cloth. If you want an alternate theory, maybe the Professor changed his mind about sharing his story with us and arranged his own kidnapping. Maybe he's already back home in Thailand."

"Think what you want, but don't be surprised if we learn that the Professor was spirited aboard a tramp steamer bound for Shanghai."

"Well, if you are right, let's hope he's in a comfortable cabin and not inside a 55-gallon steel drum."

"Now look who is being the pessimist." Roger stood up when he heard Melanie's bedroom door open. She had a smile on her face as she approached the couple. "You spoke with Mister Bancroft?"

"Yes. He was very sympathetic. I explained that it's been nearly five days and neither the local authorities nor the Virginia State Police have any information about my father's current whereabouts. He thought he could use that fact to argue that my father is no longer in the State, which could bring the FBI into the case. Mister Bancroft has a friend in the FBI Director's Office and promised to talk to her today."

"That is certainly encouraging news," offered Amanda.

"Yes, it is. I just hope they can do something quickly. Mister Bancroft suggested that the men who took my father may be taking him back to China; probably by ship."

Roger looked over at Amanda and winked.

CHAPTER TWENTY-FOUR

The Jordan Valley
3 Months after the Arrival

THE SCOUT SHIP COMMANDER and his two weapons specialists accompanied by Marlot arrived at the walled city more than one hour before darkness would begin to descend on the city. Along the way the three Visitors peppered Marlot with questions: *Besides the Main Gate, are there any other entrances to the city?* "Yes, the East Gate. It is on the opposite side of the city from the Main Gate." *What about a secret tunnel or other hidden entrance?* "There is a natural spring on the inside that sometimes washes out the earth below the wall, creating a breech. If it has not been attended to recently, a man can easily squeeze through the opening." *What weapons are we likely to face if we can get inside?* "Knives and swords." *Where might they be holding our people?* "I don't know, but maybe I can find out."

A contingent of men in the parapet observed with concerned interest as Marlot and the three Visitors approached the Main Gate of the city. When they were still fifty meters from the gate, Marlot spoke up. "Why don't you three wait here and allow me to speak to the Elder and try to negotiate the release of your crewmen?"

"This is not your concern, Marlot," objected the Commander.

"Yes, but if it can be settled peacefully and your people are released without harm, isn't that the best outcome?" The other two Visitors murmured in agreement.

The Commander considered Marlot's argument for several seconds before replying. "Maybe it is the best course of action for now. Even if you cannot negotiate a release, perhaps you can learn where they are holding our people. But," he added forcefully, "we won't wait too long." The Commander pointed up at the first quarter moon still high in the western sky. "We will wait at the tree line. If you do not return with a negotiated solution by the time the moon is down, we will proceed with a plan of our own."

The Visitors sat on the ground and watched as Marlot proceeded toward the Main Gate. When he was within earshot of the men in the parapet, he raised his right hand to signify that his intentions were peaceful and called up to the men. "Open the gate and allow me to enter and speak with the Elder regarding the Visitors."

When the gate opened briefly and Marlot disappeared behind it, the Visitors retreated to a stand of cedars a few hundred meters from their former position and opposite the north wall of the city. Earlier, Marlot had described the location on the north wall where they might possibly find the entrance breech, if it existed at all.

"I AM HERE, YOUR REVERENCE, to learn why it is that you have taken the two Visitors captive, and what are your demands regarding them?" In the meeting he requested with the City Elder, Marlot tried to present himself as a neutral party whose sole objective was a peaceful solution to the problem at hand.

The Elder replied, "Before I answer your question, can you tell us — why are you here representing the interests of the Visitors? Are you with them, or are you with us?"

Marlot hesitated before answering the Elder's question. "It is true that my family and I have come to this place from the East, but know that we consider ourselves to be citizens of this land. We believe it was the will of the Lord God that we are here. And we also believe that God would have us live in peace with both neighbors and strangers alike. The Visitors have come here in peace. They are explorers, desiring only to learn about us and this land. They have told me that after a time, they will leave this place, never to return."

"You have a reputation as a wise and wealthy man, Marlot, but the Visitors have deceived you. You have seen them exhibit great power and knowledge, but not as gifts from the Lord God, but from Beelzebub himself. Look upon their hands.

With just four digits they are like double cloven hooves. And their females not only dress in a manner indistinguishable from the men, but appear to possess the same stature as the men instead of serving them as is ordained by the Lord God."

"Then what, may I ask, is your will concerning all of the Visitors?"

"That they be destroyed and their bodies burned along with all of their goods, and the ashes scattered to the four winds."

The apparent intransigence of the Elder was exactly what Marlot hoped not to hear. Was there no chance for a compromise? *No*, he was told. What if the Visitors agreed to leave our land now? *It is the will of the Lord God that they be destroyed.*

Marlot had but one remaining argument he could make. "The Visitors have weapons of great power, as you have witnessed. There will be much loss of life in the event of armed conflict with them."

The Elder, undaunted by Marlot's warning, folded his arms across his chest before declaring, "At dawn, two hundred men will mount an attack upon the three Visitors if they are discovered outside the city wall. After they are vanquished, we will march on the Visitor encampment and subdue them. Any survivors will be brought back to the City and stoned, along with the two prisoners. By the end of the day, there will be no evidence that the Visitors dared to ever come to our land."

The Elder correctly reasoned that it would be foolish to allow the enemy to learn of the battle plans before the battle started. Consequently, Marlot was admonished not to step beyond the walls of the city — upon pain of death — until after the dawn attack on the Visitors would begin.

"May I at least be permitted to see the prisoners?"

"As you wish."

THE CLOUDS HUGGING THE WESTERN horizon appeared to glow from within — still illuminated by the moon that had set only minutes earlier — when the three Visitors began their careful advance toward the east wall of the city. They did not expect to see Marlot after his meeting with the city Elder and so they had spent the last few hours resting and carefully planning the assault they would make on the city in order to free their two crew members.

At this late hour the city was asleep. It was eerily quiet, and aside from a few scattered oil lamps, the city was dark. The Visitors felt their way along the wall for several meters until they noticed the soil damp under their feet. The region of the wall that Marlot described had to be very close.

For a few brief weeks during the rainy season each year the spring water would gather in a pool on the inside of the wall until built-up water pressure forced a breech in the earth below the stone blocks of the wall, draining the pool. And each year after the rains, some men of the city would *eventually* be assigned to repair the breech. Had this season's repair order been issued yet? Apparently not. When the Commander briefly illuminated the base of the wall with his utility light, he confirmed the presence of the gap where the water had pushed the earth away. He peered upward from under the large block of stone and judged that the opening was large enough to pass through; then signaled for the other men to follow before climbing through to the other side of the wall.

CHAPTER TWENTY-FIVE

Wilmington, Delaware
Present Day

THE PORT AT WILMINGTON was the third stop for the team of Federal officers in search of Professor Tsum and the men who had abducted him. They had spent the previous day at Norfolk and Newport News looking for Chinese-flagged vessels with a scheduled departure date within the next week. They had found only one: a ship in Norfolk loaded with raw cotton and tobacco and bound for Macau. The Captain was cooperative, allowing the officers to board and examine the contents of the hold. And when an examination of the ship's manifest revealed that the Captain's paperwork was in order, he was thanked for his cooperation and the Federal officers left the ship.

At Wilmington, there were three possible candidate vessels. The *Tian Zhou* was first on their list, scheduled to get underway the next day. The security guard on the main deck asked to see identification and then sent his assistant to find the Captain, believed to be in his stateroom.

"MY NAME IS CAPTAIN YU. How may I help you gentlemen?" Yu was middle-aged, short in stature and nearly bald. The lead agent stepped forward and displayed his badge.

"I am Agent Dawson. We have it on good authority that there is a ship here in Wilmington that may be transporting high technology electronics in violation of U.S. Export Control Laws." *Sometimes a lie is called for during the initial stage of an investigation.* "We would like permission to search your vessel."

"We carry only lumber, bound for Caracas. I can show you manifest, if you wish."

"Then you won't mind if we conduct a search? It won't take long. Then we can cross you off our list."

"I am sorry, but as you can see, we prepare to get underway soon—in morning. To bring your men aboard at this time would be big problem. Unless you have . . ." The Captain hesitated, unsure of the right word. His security guard whispered it in his ear. "Yes, warrant. Unless you have warrant, I must ask you to leave my ship."

Denying permission for a search was a red flag. "We can get a warrant, if you wish, Captain. However, when I advise the Port Director that a search warrant is pending, he will stay your departure until the warrant is issued and the search is complete. If everything is found to be in order, you should be able to get underway in a few days—a week at most."

"One whole week delay?" Captain Yu was not happy and muttered something in Mandarin to his security guard. He looked directly at Agent Dawson and spoke, "OK. Hong-Li here will escort you aroun' the ship, but please to make it quick, thank you." Yu turned away without another word and headed toward the bridge. Hong-Li motioned for the four Federal officers to step forward.

"AS YOU CAN SEE, we carry wood from trees." The ship's hold was full of milled construction lumber; stacks of it secured with steel banding and resting on pallets fashioned from larger timbers. At Agent Dawson's request Hong-Li led the search team around the entire perimeter of the ship's hold. Looking between the rows of pallets, it became obvious that if Professor Tsum was being held aboard this ship, he wasn't in the hold.

"Thanks, Hong-Li. Now we need to see the rest of the ship." Next stop was the engine room. Although not suitable as living quarters for anyone once the ship was underway, it could serve as a place to stow someone temporarily while in port. But they found no one in the engine room of the *Tian Zhou*.

The ship had four small guest cabins located forward, below the bridge deck. Hong-Li fumbled with a ring of keys until he found the right one for the first cabin. "The guest rooms are all empty. You won't find any illegal goods here, but I will open every one for you," Hong-Li added. With tightly-made bunks and no sign of personal effects, it was clear that the first three cabins were unassigned. But a spiral notebook rested on the surface of the small writing desk in the fourth cabin and the double bunk appeared to have been hastily made.

"Where is the occupant of this stateroom?" asked Agent Dawson.

"It is a couple from South America. On honeymoon, I think. They are in the town for today, but will return tonight." In looking about the cabin, Agent Dawson took particular notice that the wardrobe cabinet, with just few articles of clothing, included nothing that might be worn by a woman.

In the passageway outside the guest cabin Hong-Li announced the next stop on the search. "We go aft to crew quarters, but please to understand that third shift crew will be still sleeping at this time, so it will be dark." Hong-Li led the way with the officers following behind — Agent Dawson last.

"We'll try to be very quiet," offered one of the officers.

The crew's sleeping compartment contained two rows of bunks stacked three-high with a narrow aisle between the rows, but only seven of the eighteen bunks were occupied. Even in the dim light, it was clear that the sleeping crewmen were quite young — in their twenties or thirties — judging from the muscular bodies and black mops of hair without a trace of grey. That is, except for one of the men. He was very thin and although his face was turned away toward the bulkhead, the ball cap that he wore could not mask his clearly advanced age. *This was no crewman.*

As the group moved toward the far end of the compartment, Agent Dawson stopped at the middle bunk occupied by the elderly gentleman. "Professor Tsum!" he whispered. The man turned his head, looked directly at Dawson and mouthed a reply — *Yes!* — and nodded. Without warning, Agent Dawson was knocked off his feet by a man jumping out of the bunk below the Professor.

"Halt!" yelled one of the agents. He and the others gave chase, stepping carefully over Agent Dawson sprawled on the floor of the compartment. By the time they reached the open door to the passageway and looked about, the fugitive had disappeared. The agents found their way out to the Main Deck after a wrong turn or two and just in time to see the man vanish into a crowd of tourists waiting to board a cruise ship on the far side of the wharf.

CHAPTER TWENTY-SIX

The Jordan Valley
3 Months after the Arrival

THE THREE VISITORS FOUND THEMSELVES inside the city wall, looking about for a clue as to where their fellow crew members were being held captive. The city was asleep and they had made a silent entry through the breech in the wall. And so they were surprised by the figure moving toward them in the darkness. The Commander raised his weapon, just as the figure spoke up.

"It is me — Marlot," the figure called out to the Visitors in a loud whisper.

"What are you doing here, Marlot?"

"When I was forbidden to leave the city after speaking with the Elder, I knew you would try to make entry here. I have been waiting in the granary," Marlot pointed to a building about twenty meters away, "over there. Come with me now. It is a safe place where we can speak without alerting anyone from the city."

The granary was a large single story stone structure with a low roof. The roof was well-sealed against the elements with overlapping tiles arranged over hewn wooden beams — important because of the need to prevent the growth of mold due to moisture. This communal store of grain was the primary source of sustenance for the population of the city for the several months between harvests. The granary housed more than a hundred large pottery jars with about half of them empty. The remaining grain would need to last for several months until the next harvest. The building also contained a number of wooden bins partially filled with dried apricots, pomegranates and apples.

The citizens of the city were allowed a meager daily ration of grain and dried fruit to supplement their personal stores of food. Except for a few hours each day that distribution of provisions occurred, the granary was unattended. It was understood that anyone found guilty of stealing would be put to death by stoning.

Marlot and the three Visitors sat on the earthen floor of the granary, facing each other. The Scout Ship Commander asked Marlot about his meeting with the Elder.

"He is a very stubborn man, and unwilling to negotiate for the release of your people. I feared from the beginning that he would be uncooperative."

"Because?"

"Because under his leadership strangers in this land have always been dealt with harshly. Many who have tried to settle here have been killed along with their families. It was only because I had sufficient wealth to pay a large tribute that my people have not been harmed and we have been permitted to stay. He has stirred the people against you by declaring that you are devils and have been sent here by the Chief Devil, Beelzebub."

"Ridiculous!"

"Yes, but know that he intends grave harm to you and all your people. He plans even to mount an attack on your encampment tomorrow."

"What were you able to learn about our crew members being held?"

"I was able to see them. Both are injured, but not gravely. They are being held under guard, not far from here."

"Show us."

MARLOT LED THE VISITORS outside and along the rear wall of the granary. Crouching low to the ground, he pointed to a burning oil lamp, visible on the second level of a building four structures away from their present position. "They are being held in a room at the top of the stone stairway. When I was there earlier, I saw two guards outside the door. If they are asleep now, it should be easy to overpower them. But the problem is that there are many of the Elder's men sleeping nearby. If they hear a disturbance, they will come running."

"We need a diversion," declared the Commander. "Are there any wooden structures a little distance from here? Structures that will burn?"

"Many of the houses of the citizens are built with wood."

"What about an empty building? I don't wish to harm innocent women and children."

"Yes. There is a large wooden structure where the Elder meets with his men. I can take you there."

Before setting out with Marlot, the Commander told the other two Visitors to wait until the diversion attracted the guards and the Elder's men nearby, then to free the prisoners and take them out of the city through the breech in the wall. He would join up with them along the way, or back at their encampment.

"LISTEN, MARLOT. You must find your family and any of your people and flee the city tonight. If the wind should gain strength, the fire may spread to other parts of the city. And if the Elder suspects that you have helped us, he may harm you and your family. Thank you for your help, but for your own safety you must leave."

The two men were at the structure that Marlot had described. The wooden timbers and roof shingles were so dry that it appeared as if a single spark could set it ablaze. Several other structures that stood dangerously close were potentially at risk as well.

"I am troubled, Commander, that you would proceed with your plan after expressing concern for the well-being of the women and children. Would you risk the destruction of the city if you believed there were just fifty righteous people living here?"

"I have come to believe that this city is corrupt to the core, but I wish no harm to come to the people. I do only what is necessary to assure the safety of my crew members. But go and find the righteous where you can and urge them to leave so that they will be spared should the flames begin to spread. I will wait just one half hour before setting the torch to this structure."

CHAPTER TWENTY-SEVEN

MELANIE TSUM HEEDED THE ADVICE from the police detective and relocated to a different hotel—one outside of Alexandria. The Professor was safe and the reunion with his daughter was a joyous one, but the men who had abducted Professor Tsum were still out there.

No one—not even the Captain of the *Tian Zhou*—could be charged in the case. Yes, it was true that he had accepted a two-thousand dollar cash payment for safe passage to Venezuela for an unknown Chinese national and his elderly travel companion, but he denied having any knowledge that the Professor was being held against his will. The FBI determined there was insufficient evidence to bring charges against the Captain, and the *Tian Zhou* was allowed to leave port after only a forty-eight hour delay.

At the urging of the detective from Alexandria, the Chief of Police from Fairfax County agreed to provide some limited police protection for the

Tsums. A police cruiser dispatched from the McLean District Station would patrol the vicinity of the hotel for the next several days, and an officer promised to come by the hotel suite to check on them frequently.

Melanie wanted her father to rest for another day after his ordeal, but the Professor wouldn't hear of it. "I am fine," he insisted. "Please ask Miss Marshall and Professor Atwood to come today; there is much more we have to tell them."

"THANK YOU FOR SUPPORT you provided to my daughter during my recent absence."

"I wish we could have done more," offered Roger. "It was difficult for her; especially after hearing nothing from the local authorities in the first few days—until the FBI got involved."

"Once I was taken to ship and placed in cabin with one of the gang members, I believed I would never see my daughter again."

Amanda asked the question that they had speculated about since the Professor's disappearance. "Were you ever told what they wanted from you? Why did they take you?"

"I was told only that I was being taken to Beijing. But..." Professor paused before continuing, "It was an unpleasant experience that I have put in the past."

It was clear to Amanda that Professor Tsum did not wish to recount the events of the past few days. She took the discussion in a different direction.

"Professor, when we were last together you were telling us about Professor Chu and his time in the mountain village that James Hilton, the author, had told him about."

"Yes, Professor Chu spent several years in the village. That was not his original intention, but the war with Japan was expanding. Many more cities in China come under Japanese occupation. After the United States entered the war, it was hoped that soon the Japanese would be defeated, and Professor Chu decided to wait out the war in the peaceful village, away from the fighting. No one thought war would last so long until 1945.

"Professor Chu married a young woman from the village and they had a daughter. If you recall from last week, I was about to tell you something important before I was taken away." Before continuing, Professor Tsum paused and looked over at Melanie. "It is simply that Melanie is not my natural daughter. She was born in that mountain village, daughter of Professor Chu and his wife."

"How? Why?" Roger didn't know exactly what to ask following this startling revelation.

"Meiko—Melanie's Chinese given name—was only eleven years old when Professor Chu was arrested. Melanie's mother died several years earlier, not long after they leave mountain village. The doctors say she was afflicted with Progeria—the premature aging disease. Two days before he was arrested, Professor Chu brought his daughter to our home and begged us to care for her as our own until he might be released — if ever. Naturally, we agreed. Melanie was a sweet child, and we had no children of our own."

"And your wife cared for Melanie when you were sent to the collective farm?"

"Yes, but because my family had to move, we lost contact with the Professor. He did not know where his daughter was living until I was able to meet with him in Beijing after my release. It was good that they were able to spend some time together before Chu pass away later that year." Melanie wiped tears from her eyes as Professor Tsum spoke of her birth father. "My daughter was a student at Beijing Language Institute, but she transferred to the University when classes resumed there and I was reinstated in my teaching position."

CHAPTER TWENTY-EIGHT

The Jordan Valley
Three Months and One Day after the Arrival

THE DECISION TO LEAVE the Jordan Valley was an easy one for the Scout Ship Commander. In the three months since their arrival the Visitors made just one friend — and hundreds of enemies — among the locals. As had been feared, the diversionary fire started by the Commander spread quickly due to fierce night winds that came up suddenly and turned the walled city into an inferno. Despite Marlot's warnings to flee, more than a hundred of the city inhabitants had perished in the fires and a dozen more were killed while attempting to stop the Visitors during the successful rescue of their comrades and escape from the city.

Marlot arrived at the Visitor's encampment with his two daughters at mid-morning and brought the bad news that Ado — his wife — was missing. "I don't understand," he explained. "We had reached a safe place beyond the walls of the city when suddenly she stopped and turned back toward the East Gate. I tried to reason with her but she would not listen.

No one has seen her since and I fear my Ado has perished."

"I am so sorry, Marlot. Is there something I can say or do to comfort you? I fear I have destroyed the only friendship we have made in this place."

But Marlot held no resentment against the Commander. "Perhaps it was the will of God," he said.

IT WOULD HAVE BEEN OBVIOUS to even the most casual observer that the Visitors were preparing for an immediate departure.

"Where will you go?" asked Marlot.

"To that place you told us about—in the West. You called it 'Egypt'. And for your own safety and that of your daughters, you should come with us and leave this place forever. There are many from the city who would do you harm just because you have befriended us."

"Thank you for your kind offer, but my extended family—including my uncle—still we are respected in this region, and the Elder and many of his supporters perished in the fire. We will not be harmed. And I must search for my dear wife, whether or not she still lives."

MARLOT AND HIS TWO DAUGHTERS watched with astonishment as the scout ship slowly rose from the ground—a vertical ascent—powered by the pair of auxiliary air breathing engines running on a chemically-altered supply of the hydrazine rocket fuel that had propelled the vessel out of earth orbit toward the surface three months earlier. They watched until the vessel disappeared over the horizon in the direction of the gray column of smoke that was visible from the encampment.

The Mission Commander aboard the mother ship was highly disturbed to learn of the events of the preceding day. "Was there no other means to secure the release of our people," he asked, "without burning down the entire city?" It was not until the Scout Ship Commander submitted a detailed report explaining the need for the diversionary fire that the Mission Commander acknowledged that the course of action was probably necessary. In the official report, the destruction of the city was recorded as a tragic accident.

The pilot of the scout ship eased up on the throttle and reduced altitude as the ship approached the walled city. The Commander wanted to visually verify Marlot's report of the devastation, and the Mission Commander aboard the mother ship requested some high resolution images to include in the Scout Commander's report.

The outside wall of the city was still intact, but most of the structures within were reduced to rubble. Groups of people were gathered outside the Main Gate and East Gate — a few hundred in total — waiting for the smoldering remains of their homes to cool enough to allow them to scavenge for personal goods that might have survived the flames. The Commander felt a twinge of regret in the pit of his stomach from the sight of the granary below. The roof was collapsed, revealing what had once been an orderly array of pottery jars full of grain; now just a disarrangement of broken and blackened shards. The next several months would be hard on the survivors of this city.

The ship and its crew made one final pass over the wreckage of the city and its former inhabitants and headed west, oblivious to the human wave of shaking fists and angry curses sent in their direction. But elsewhere on the Plain of Jordan it was generally believed that the inhabitants of the walled city had only themselves to blame for the destruction, delivered due to their iniquity by the hand of an angry God.

FROM THE SURVEYS conducted by the mother ship from earth orbit and the description of the region related by Marlot earlier, the Scout Ship Commander estimated that their destination was about 500 kilometers to the west. This is distance that the scout ship could have covered in little more than an hour, but the helmsman was told to set a more leisurely pace at low altitude to provide the crew with a bird's eye view of the territory.

They passed over the north end of the Dead Sea — the inland "lake" they had first explored upon their arrival; then over Hebron, the place where Marlot's uncle had settled after leaving Egypt. Further west, the land appeared less hospitable, with great expanses of sand dunes separated by low lying dry lakebeds displaying the grayish-white evidence of salinization. The Great Sea to the north probably covered much of the region when the planet was young. There was little vegetation and absolutely no sign of human life in this extensive, arid region of the earth that would come to be known as the Sinai Desert.

But the view below began to change as they continued further west; a few small settlements at first, then some larger ones. More and more of the land appeared to be under cultivation, and soon they came upon the Great River that Marlot had told them about, flowing north to the sea.

THE WIDE RIVER was dotted with small islands; barren and unoccupied because waters of the Great River would completely cover them during the spring arrival of the floods that Marlot had spoken of. For reasons of security, the Scout Ship Commander selected one with a narrow land bridge to the shoreline and the ship descended to earth. If the inhabitants of Egypt proved no more hospitable than those from their previous host country, the Visitors could make a safe and speedy escape.

The Scout Ship Commander and three of his crew members disembarked from their vessel and proceeded toward the land bridge. Each carried a side arm. Two of the remaining four Visitors would maintain a security detail outside the ship; the other two were left to monitor the systems aboard the vessel so that a quick departure could be effected if found necessary.

A contingent of locals made their appearance on the shore. There were ten men, all but one carrying a spear or sword and a shield, and each similarly dressed. They marched to the apron of land on the shore side of the land bridge and stood at attention. The Commander moved forward on to the land bridge, leaving his three armed crew members behind. In a similar move, the unarmed leader of the contingent of ten — the Captain of the Guard — walked toward him; the two men facing each other at the center of the bridge.

The Commander raised an open right hand in greeting. They exchanged some words, spoken by each in a non-threatening tone. And although neither could fully understand what the other was saying, the Commander sensed that foremost on the mind of the Captain of the Guard was an answer to the question, *"From where have you come?"*

The Commander lowered himself on to one knee and using a short stick he found nearby, began to draw in the damp, packed sand. He first marked an "x" near the feet of the local leader, then drew a crescent moon and a larger circle surrounded by rays depicting the sun a short distance away. He then stepped a few paces beyond the images and crouched down, dragging the stick along the surface in a continuous line, passing between the images of the sun and moon and extending it all the way to the "x". Then he stood facing the other man and brushed the sand from his hands.

The local leader turned toward his men on the shore and shouted an order. They immediately lowered their weapons and shields and stood at ease. He gestured for the Commander to follow him and that the three Visitors at the island end of the land bridge should come as well. The Commander issued the order and the four Visitors joined the contingent of locals, all headed in the direction of the sprawling city lying nearby.

CHAPTER TWENTY-NINE

Bayan Har Mountains, China
3 Years after the Arrival

DURING THE PRECEDING EIGHTEEN months, much had changed—and much remained the same—for the inhabitants and Visitors in the environs of the Bayan Har Mountains. The local population was now divided into two factions. The farmers and herdsmen in the countryside had developed a strong alliance with the Visitors, mutually benefiting each other. The Visitors helped develop the water supply and taught improved farming techniques that enormously increased crop yields. The Medical Officer from the ship conducted weekly clinics for the locals and trained several promising candidates in the treatment of common injuries and ailments. The country locals reciprocated by providing the Visitors with foodstuffs.

But inside the village, the distrust and contempt for the Visitors had grown, thanks to the influence of the young chief, Zhang Zhu, and pressure from his minions. On one level, the hatred that Zhu held for the Visitors was understandable. When they first arrived, it was clear that the old Chieftain's health was in decline. His son was next in line to become Chief and already had a reputation for throwing his weight around—making life difficult for many of the locals. He reveled in the power that he had and looked forward to the day when he would have it all.

But after the Arrival, the focus of the local population shifted quickly to the Visitors. They had come from the stars and possessed near-magical powers and wondrous devices. How could Zhu compete with these nearly godlike men and women? Zhang Zhu often lamented to his thug minions, *"Why did the Visitors have to come to my mountain?"*

After several unsuccessful initiatives to come to an accommodation with Zhu and his people, the Visitors were resigned to the notion that a state of uneasy tension between them would likely exist until the Visitors left the Bayan Har region. They hoped that any violent confrontation could be avoided.

On a happier note, there was a big change for Landon and Jia-Li with the birth of their daughter, Hui-Ying. The little girl brought a great deal of joy to all the Visitors whenever her mother brought her to the scout ship.

THE COMMUNICATIONS from the mother ship that the Visitors at Bayan Har were able to intercept were less frequent now. Months of monitoring failed to provide any indication that the Mission Commander had changed his opinion regarding the status of their "lost" ship. It was still considered to be a tragic event of the past — and best left there.

Monitoring the communications finally shed light on one earlier source of confusion: The Visitors at Bayan Har knew that the intended destination of second scout ship was the Jordan Valley, but the communications intercepted from the mother ship suggested a different location. Eventually they were able to surmise that the Scout Ship Commander had relocated to an alternate location further west due to hostile encounters with the local population.

"I KEEP THINKING THERE MUST BE some way we can signal them." Kandra, the chemical engineer from the ship wondered out loud as she watched the mother ship high in the sky overhead — something that she had witnessed numerous times before. Landon and Kandra had just finished listening to the last set of recorded transmissions from the mother ship.

"I don't know what else we can do," offered Landon. "We can't even generate a radio signal, thanks to — well, you know why."

"What about a light signal?"

"How many signal fires have we tried? There must be thousands of outdoor fires burning on the surface of this planet as we speak, and many visible from space. No one up there is paying attention to fires."

"No, I mean a beam of light or a light reflection that we could aim at the mother ship as it passes overhead — like right now. The sun is nearly set, so the sky overhead is dark enough for the mother ship to be seen, and if we had a big enough mirror, we might be able to signal the ship with light reflected from the sun before it sets."

"That might work if we had a giant mirror. Let me think about it."

CHAPTER THIRTY

Giza, Egypt
2570 BC

EGYPT HAD EVOLVED TO BECOME a significant civilization well before the arrival of the Visitors. Archaeological evidence reveals that early Egyptians were hunting, fishing and using stone tools as early as 12,000 BC. Cattle herding was common in southwest Egypt near the border of what is now Sudan by 8000 BC. But it is near that date that natural climate change began to alter the trajectory of Egyptian history. Over the next 5,000 years Egypt became progressively dryer. The Sahara Desert covered much of the region and the formerly scattered population became concentrated around the Nile Valley. Each year, melting snow from the mountains of East Africa became a rush of water overflowing the banks of the river, depositing a layer of topsoil—rich in nutrients—that provided farmers with abundant crops of grains and vegetables. Typically, the floods began in late spring and continued until September with the growing season from October to February. Harvesting began in February and continued until the next cycle of flooding began.

The annual harvests were so important to the population that sacks of grain served as the common medium of exchange until the introduction of coinage 600 BC. Egyptian farmers also grew a wide variety of vegetables, raised cattle, sheep, goats, pigs, all types of poultry and even domesticated bees for the production of honey and wax.

The first Egyptian hieroglyphic writing and use of copper tools date from about 3000 BC, a time corresponding to a political division of the country with Lower Egypt in the North and Upper Egypt in the South. Papyrus documents began to appear a few hundred years later.

Early Egyptians had an understanding of many modern mathematical concepts, often applying them to the keeping of books of account for trade and commerce. The number system was decimal-based and arithmetic operations of addition, subtraction, multiplication and division were well understood. They could express numbers as powers of ten and compute areas of various geometrical shapes.

THE FOUR VISITORS were escorted to the Palace of Pharaoh Khufu. They were greeted outside the granite building by the Pharaoh's vizier Kawab, who also happened to be the eldest son of Khufu. After conferring privately with the Captain of the Guard for a few minutes, Kawab brought the

Visitors into the Receiving Chamber and seated them at a stone bench facing a raised platform. Two wooden chairs rested on the platform — one rather plain and one that was ornately carved with the seat back and bottom upholstered in purple fabric. The chairs were unoccupied.

The Receiving Chamber was square, about ten meters on a side with a high ceiling. A series of narrow vertical openings high on two of the walls let in some daylight from outside, but the source of most of the dim illumination in the room came from more than a dozen oil lamps mounted on the walls and two more on stanchions placed on either side of the wooden chairs on the platform. Colorful drawings of animals and people in agricultural scenes adorned the walls.

There were several men and women seated about the room behind the stone bench. Most were elegantly dressed — at least in contrast to the simple garments worn by the ordinary citizens the Visitors encountered on their way to the palace. The women's eyes were heavily made up in blue and green shades; their hair straight and jet black. Two of the men were seated at a wooden table with writing instruments and scrolls — probably papyrus — and an oil lamp on the table between them. The strangely dressed Visitors instantly received the undivided attention of everyone in the room.

Kawab disappeared into an anteroom behind the raised platform and returned several minutes later following an imposing figure of a man dressed in a flowing purple robe trimmed in gold embroidery. Every Egyptian in the room stood at attention as soon as Pharaoh entered the chamber, and the four Visitors immediately followed their lead. Khufu and his vizier son seated themselves in the platform chairs and Kawab gestured for everyone in the room to sit.

For the next twenty minutes, the Visitors answered questions — to the extent they could be understood — posed by the Pharaoh. Not directly, of course, for it was forbidden to address Pharaoh in that way. Instead, Pharaoh would whisper his question to the vizier who would direct it to the Visitors and after the response, repeat the answer back to Khufu.

Pharaoh Khufu was impressed that the Visitors had come from such a long distance, and he hoped to see the vessel that had brought them here. They were welcome to stay as long as they wished, and Kawab would assign a security detail to escort them whenever they came to the city.

Before returning to the scout ship, the Captain of the Guard and the vizier took the Visitors to a construction project about a kilometer from the Palace. It was an impressive sight due to its sheer size. The base of the unfinished structure was a huge square, more than 200 meters on each side made up of closely fitting blocks of limestone. There were several courses of stone blocks set upon one another, each slightly shorter than the one below it. The vizier explained using a sketch in the dirt that the final shape was to be a four-sided pyramid.

The site was about two and one-half kilometers from the Nile and a canal had been dug from the river to a point near the base of the unfinished pyramid. Hundreds of men could be seen dragging a block of limestone or granite, perhaps weighing as much as seventy tons, off of a barge and on to the land near the base of the structure. Other crews were moving the huge stone blocks to the current structure and up inclined ramps of packed earth, pulling on dozens of ropes tied to each block.

It was impossible to guess how many workers were involved. The vizier told them that including the men that worked in the quarries and those transporting the blocks of stone and placing them in their final position, as many as 40,000 workers were engaged in the project at any one time. The vizier emphasized that these were paid workers, not slaves.

The limestone came from quarries across the river, while the granite blocks that were used for the royal burial chamber on the inside of the structure were transported by barge from Aswan, more than 800 kilometers distant. In the quarries, the blocks were cut out by creating deep grooves in the stone using copper chisels, then pounding wooden wedges deep into the grooves. When the wood was soaked with water, the wedges would expand, fracturing the stone.

The vizier explained that at this point in time, the project was less than half complete. The structure had risen to a height of almost fifty meters with another hundred meters to go. The stepped structure of the pyramid walls would eventually be completely covered with polished limestone in a veneer-like treatment. A single course of the beautiful polished stone had already been fitted to one of the four sides of the base.

DURING THE NEXT FOUR YEARS, the Visitors and the locals, both the common people and their rulers, developed and maintained a peaceful and mutually respectful relationship. The Visitors made frequent side trips within the region, including north to the Great (Mediterranean) Sea. Their personal safety was always guaranteed by written decree of the Pharaoh with letters of introduction sent ahead in advance of their travel.

It would be ten more years, long after the departure of the Visitors, before the Great Pyramid of Giza was finished and another century would pass before two more pyramids and the Great Sphinx would rise above the Giza Plateau on the West Bank of the Nile. The Great Pyramid, planned before the arrival of the Visitors and executed without their assistance, would stand as the tallest man-made structure on earth for the next 3,800 years. Today it remains a testament to the skill of the artisans and the devotion of the workers to their

Pharaoh — and undeniable evidence of the greatness of that ancient Egyptian civilization.

CHAPTER THIRTY-ONE

McLean, Virginia
Present Day

"WHEN THE CULTURAL REVOLUTION was over and I was at University in Beijing once again, it was a much better time in China. But for me, it did not last too long. The problem started with a book called *Chariots of the Gods*. It was published in 1968 by a Swiss man, Erich von Däniken. You have heard of the man and his book, I am sure."

"Yes, of course we have," replied Amanda.

"Then you know that in that book, he claimed there were many examples in history of extraterrestrials visiting earth. Many believe that much of what he wrote was only fiction, but millions of books were sold and the idea of ancient astronauts captured imagination of the public.

"I had been back at University for one year when I began to receive inquiries about the paper that Professor Chu and I publish in 1956. Many made requests to come to University to interview me, but all were denied. It was repeated situation of what happened more than ten years earlier: University was under pressure from unhappy Chinese government officials and warned me there would be big problem for me if inquiries continued."

"But it was not your fault," protested Amanda. You weren't the author of the book that caused all the renewed interest in ancient astronauts."

"That is exactly what I told the Dean at University, but he did not care. He had Chinese translation of von Däniken's book, and as I sat in his office he read from it stories claiming extraterrestrial help with Egyptian pyramids and statues of Easter Island and much more. After reading each story, he would shout at me.

"I argue that my research about the Dropa Stones was very thorough and credible. He didn't care what I said; he was angry and threw that book at me. When finally he became more calm, he suggested that maybe I should go away for a time. Maybe he could arrange a sabbatical for me in Thailand. One week later, I leave for Bangkok, to Silpakorn University.

"Soon after arriving in Bangkok, I decide that I will never return to China, and so I have my wife and Melanie ask for permission to travel to Hong Kong for shopping. Instead, they fly from Hong Kong to Bangkok to join me. I was happy to take teaching position at the school in Department of Oriental Languages."

"What about the Dropa Disc? How did you get it out of China?"

"It was easy. I carry it in my luggage. Not so much scrutiny back then as there is today."

CHAPTER THIRTY-TWO

Bayan Har Mountains, China
4 Years after the Arrival

THE PAST YEAR HAD BEEN a prosperous one for many members of the local population at Bayan Har. Before leaving permanently for Chiang-Ri, the ship's geologist had identified several veins of galena — a lead ore that was rich in silver — while exploring a canyon near the village. He demonstrated how a smelting process could separate the silver from the lead and many local farmers spent the next few months after the last harvest mining and smelting. Periodically, they would transport their silver down the mountain to a market center near the Yalong River where it could be traded for tools, fabrics and other supplies. The silver from Bayan Har was highly prized by the river people. The farmers-turned-miners also traded with a jewelry craftsman — a silversmith — in the local village at Bayan Har. This man had a reputation for creating some stunningly beautiful objects of art and silver jewelry, often inlaid with jade.

When Landon saw some examples of the man's work, he thought of how much Jia-Li would appreciate a fine piece of jewelry. He asked the Scout Ship Commander if he might appropriate one of the remaining gold bars that were stored in the ship's vault. One had been given to the village chief as a token of friendship shortly after the Arrival, but it was unlikely that the remaining bars would be needed. Landon was given a gold ingot that weighed nearly a kilogram and carried it with him when he went to see the silversmith.

"I AM LANDON. What is your name?" The smith looked up from his workbench just inside the doorway of the small shop. Two very large black male dogs rose from their prone position on the floor behind the workbench, tracking the Visitor's every movement with their eyes. *Must be guard animals*, he thought.

Heat from the forge in the corner kept the shop a little too warm for Landon's comfort, but he supposed it would be welcome when the weather turned colder. As he looked about, Landon noticed a living area beyond the doorway at the back of the shop. This man lived where he worked.

"I have heard of you, Landon. You are one of the Visitors. My name is Ming Yu. Welcome to my shop. I get only a few customers here. Most of what I make is taken to the market at the river. Are you maybe interested in a piece of my work?" Ming Yu gestured at some open shelves behind him that held several silver pieces, including bowls, bracelets and silver-handled daggers with what looked like bluish steel blades. Many of the pieces were inlaid with jade.

It had taken Landon some time to understand the locals' interest in jewelry made from silver, considering that his home planet regarded it as a base metal of only nominal value. "Do you ever work with gold?" he asked.

Ming Yu laughed. "I see very little gold here in my shop; it is much too dear." He reached under the workbench for a small wooden box and placed it on the surface of the bench. It held five or six gold rings, and Landon examined them briefly before setting them aside. "The silver smelters sometimes bring in some gold as there is usually a small amount found in the silver ore. Maybe one part in one hundred."

"Then show me some of your finest silver amulets." Landon was playing a little mind game with the silversmith, purposely not disclosing what he was really thinking.

Ming Yu picked three pieces from the display shelving and placed them on the workbench in front of the Visitor. All three were striking. The two largest were oval shaped with much fine detail and a jade center in the form of a sea turtle on one amulet and a frog on the other. The smaller piece was shaped like a flower with four narrow petals resting on a round ring with a central jade bud. Each amulet was fitted with a loop of fine leather that had been dyed flat black.

Landon pointed at the two larger pieces and asked, "Could you make these two pieces in gold, if you had the gold?"

"Of course, but—" Before he could continue, Landon interrupted the man by pulling the gold ingot out of his jacket pocket and setting it on the workbench in front of him.

"There is certainly enough gold in this bar to make eight or ten amulets. Tell me if you are willing to agree to this trade: I give you this gold bar. You make me these two amulets, but in gold instead of silver and with a gold chain instead of leather. Also you give me this small silver amulet and one jade and silver dagger." Landon paused and looked for a reaction from Ming Yu. "What do you think, Ming Yu? Do we have a deal?"

"It is very generous offer, but there is one problem."

"What is the problem?"

"I cannot make a gold chain strong enough to hang heavy amulet around the neck. It would break; maybe after one week or one month, but eventually chain would break. I cannot even make chain from silver, which is why all these have leather loop instead of chain."

"Then I have a question. Could you make a strong chain from copper?"

"Yes, it would be no problem, but a gold amulet would not look good hanging from copper chain. I would not make or sell you such an item. "

"I agree, Ming Yu. What I want you to do is melt a mixture of copper with gold to make the chains. Maybe three parts gold to one part copper by weight. They will be nearly as strong as copper chains and look almost like pure gold; just a little more red."

Ming Yu agreed to the deal. "Take the small silver amulet and dagger with you today. Come back in ten days for the gold amulets. If you are correct about using copper with the gold, the amulets will have chains."

IN ADDITION TO THE NEWLY ESTABLISHED silver trade, there were other examples of commerce growth in the region of Bayan Har. Kandra, the chemical engineer from the ship, taught the local women how to make soap using rainwater that was allowed to pass through bins filled with hardwood ashes. The solution was collected in clay pots placed beneath the bins, and then passed through the ashes again and again until sufficiently concentrated. The liquid was thoroughly mixed with lard and allowed to harden. Then the large block was cut into smaller bars.

After a long morning helping the women make another batch of soap, Kandra returned to the crew's gazebo and sat down in one the chairs to rest. Landon joined her a few minutes later.

"Let me show you the gift I have for my daughter." Landon showed her the silver amulet.

"For Hui-Ying?"

"Yes. Do you think she will like it?"

"She may be too young to appreciate it. You might consider waiting a few more months before you give it to her. What is it made of? It looks like silver."

"Yes, silver and jade." Kandra was staring at the silver piece, thinking. Landon spoke up to get her attention. "Kandra? Are you alright?"

"I'm fine. Sorry. I was thinking about the silver. Do you remember maybe a year ago when we were talking about signaling the mother ship?"

"You mean, with a big mirror? Sure. We gave up on that idea—we have nothing that big with a reflective surface."

"What about using the composite wall panels from inside our ship? Just one would be large enough."

"We would need to add a reflective coating. How could we do that?" Landon did not want to seem pessimistic, but he couldn't see how Kandra's idea could work.

"With some silver," she said, "—and a little chemistry."

IT TOOK ONLY UNTIL NOON the next day for Kandra to gather everything she needed for the project: (1) a clump of pure silver given to her by one of the smelters. She used a hand-held power tool from the ship to shred it into flakes, then added the silver to a flask of concentrated nitric acid from the ship's laboratory until the entire solution was reduced to silver nitrate. (2) a bucket of the concentrated solution of sodium hydroxide from the soap-making process. (3) Ammonia water from the ship's laboratory and (4) a few ounces of sugar from the ship's galley, dissolved in warm water.

A crew member helped Kandra remove one of the smooth composite wall panels — about a meter wide and two meters tall — from inside the ship and place it on a flat level table outside. Following Kandra's instructions, the crew member used a pliers-like tool to bend up all four edges of the panel slightly, creating a raised rim around the entire outside edge of the panel. Kandra used a cleaning solution to remove all traces of dust, finger prints and grease from the surface, then rinsed it carefully with clean water.

By now, the entire crew had gathered to observe the activity outside the ship that was being orchestrated by Kandra. She combined the first three chemicals in a large flask, then added the sugar solution to it. Her assistant poured the entire contents of the flask over the surface of the panel. The liquid was about a centimeter deep, retained by the bent up edges of the panel.

"I know you are all curious," she told the group, "but nothing is going to happen here until we add some heat." Kandra switched on a hand-held electric heater from the laboratory and directed the hot air stream at the surface of the liquid, moving about so that the temperature might rise more uniformly.

It was twenty minutes before the group could begin to see patches of metallic silver precipitate out of the solution and deposit on the black composite substrate. After twenty more minutes, the surface of the panel was completely coated. She asked her assistant to help pour off the liquid so that the brilliant reflective surface could air dry.

Kandra looked at Landon and said, "We can try to signal the mother ship with this panel just before dusk today. It should be completely dry by then." Landon smiled and nodded.

CHAPTER THIRTY-THREE

Wu Tai Engineering
Falls Church, Virginia
Present Day

JOHN WU EMIGRATED to the United States fifteen years earlier, became a U.S. citizen and started his engineering firm in Falls Church after three years. It was a small company with just four employees but won several lucrative subcontracts with government prime contractors. John Wu's specialty was opto-electronics. He first met Professor Tsum while studying at the University of Beijing. Wu came to the United States for graduate work at MIT about the same time that the Professor left for Bangkok.

The two men stayed in contact while Wu completed his doctorate at Cambridge. It wasn't long after returning to Beijing that the engineer became unhappy with his life in China. He longed for the taste of freedom he had experienced while completing his graduate studies.

After receiving an invitation to present a paper at an important electro-optics conference in Zurich,

John Wu recognized that this was his chance to leave behind the oppressive political presence that kept him and his fellow academics in Beijing continually looking over their shoulders and worried about who might be monitoring their spoken and written words.

But there was a catch. The Chinese Government was loathe to lose its most talented citizens — especially talented scientists — and discouraged their international travel for obvious reasons. There was little risk of losing individuals with familial roots in the country because it was common knowledge that harsh consequences would certainly befall those left behind — the wives and parents of defectors. But John Wu had no close relatives in China; he was unmarried, had no siblings and both of his parents had died years before. And so his request to attend the conference in Zurich was initially denied. University officials appealed the decision, arguing that an offer to promote him to the position of Engineering Department Head would certainly assure John Wu's return to the University after the conference.

The government officials reversed their initial negative decision at the last minute and Wu was permitted to attend the conference and present his paper. It was well-received. The day before the conference ended, Wu walked to the American Consular Agency near his hotel and spoke with a consular officer about asylum and immigrating to the United States. When the electro-optics conference ended at noon the next day, John Wu was two hours out of Zurich on an American Airlines flight to Kennedy International in New York City.

"WELCOME TO WU TAI ENGINEERING." The Tsums with Amanda and Roger arrived at John Wu's facility at 9 AM. The modern, single-story brick building was nestled in the woods just off the Lee Highway. Doctor Wu greeted Professor Tsum warmly, "It has been many years, Professor. It is good to see you." Wu spoke with perfect English and not even a hint of an accent. After the introductions were completed the guests were escorted to a conference table at one end of the brightly-lit electronics lab. All eyes were focused on the round disc resting on a plastic mat at the center of the conference table.

Doctor Wu pushed the object toward Professor Tsum. "As you can see, Professor, your disc is quite safe. When the police came here and I learned that you had been abducted, we increased the security here. I was much relieved to learn that you were rescued by the authorities and that you were not harmed."

Professor Tsum acknowledged Wu's statement with a nod and slid the disc to his right so that Amanda, Roger and Melanie could get a closer view. It was just as the Professor had previously described: about eight inches in diameter and nearly an inch thick, with a central perforation and spiral groove as in the photographs—from the center and out to the edge. It was a uniform dull brown color everywhere except the edge that appeared to have a thick, clear coating.

"My father and I were encouraged, Doctor Wu, when you agreed to conduct a scientific examination of the Dropa Stone here at your facility. It has been more than fifty years since it was last studied, in Beijing." Melanie then asked the question that was also on the minds of the other three visitors. "Were you able to uncover anything new from your study of it?"

Wu replied, "I read with great interest the original report from the Engineering Department in Beijing regarding composition of the disc." Roger slid the disc toward Doctor Wu who was standing at the other side of the conference table. Wu picked up the disc as he spoke, "And I was able to indeed confirm that this object is basically ceramic, combined with an iron, nickel and cobalt alloy. But despite the modern equipment and methods available to us here—equipment and methods unimaginable to the engineering staff at Beijing—we had been unable to gain any further insight into the makeup or purpose of the disc."

"So you were able to learn nothing new about it?" From the tone of his voice and expression on his face, Professor Tsum was clearly disappointed.

"Not until three days ago," Doctor Wu added, smiling. He sat down across from his guests, placed the disc back on the table and clasped his hands together, resting them on the surface of the table. "I kept reading and rereading the transcript of the symbols engraved on the disc, from the Professor's paper — the part about *the secrets locked within, waiting to be discovered.* It became a personal challenge to me, and I wasn't about to give up. As it turned out, it is only by accident that we were able to learn more." His guests listened with rapt attention as Wu continued.

"We knew that the disc exhibited some weak magnetic properties. One evening after my staff had left I was using an external magnet to check for any variation in magnetic attraction across the surface of the disc, making notes as I worked. There was an electrical storm outside, and just as I finished making my last notation, the power went out here in the lab. It was completely dark. When I reached for the disc in front of me, I accidently knocked over the powerful neodymium magnet that I had placed on the surface of the table next to the disc. At that very instant, the disc emitted a weak flash of light. I was able to repeat the emission simply by waving the magnet close to the edge of the disc. The emitted light was not very bright, but quite visible in the darkness."

"You had to actually move the magnet near the disc to get it to emit light, not just place it nearby?" asked Roger.

"Correct. The magnetic field must pass through the disc for the light to appear. This was not an unexpected finding. That is how electronic elements usually interact with magnetic fields. But there is more, let me show you."

Doctor Wu picked up the disc once again and gestured for his visitors to accompany him to the other side of the laboratory. A strange looking mechanical apparatus was atop the work table around which they had gathered. It consisted of a belt-driven turntable and electric motor wired to a controller box. Doctor Wu placed the Dropa Disc over the vertical arbor on the turntable and slowly advanced the adjustment knob on the motor controller until the turntable began to spin. A metallic piece — assumed to be a magnet — was mounted in such a way that the edge of the rotating disc passed very close to it.

"Once this disc with its central perforation was observed to emit light when subjected to a moving magnetic field, it didn't take a stroke of genius to conclude that the disc was meant to rotate. We were able to put this apparatus together in about an hour. With the controller box, I can change the speed of rotation by adjusting the input frequency of the power to the AC motor. It's a pretty crude device, and we are assembling a far more precise direct current motor and controller, but it works.

"We can't see any of the emitted light right now because it is very faint and the ambient room light is too bright here in the lab, but if we extinguish the lights . . . ." Doctor Wu signaled for one of his associates to turn out the lights and immediately a faint band of white light about a half meter high appeared on the white wall near where they were standing.

"If you look closely, you will see that the band of light extends completely around the room." His visitors could even see a faint vestige of the light at waist-level height on their own clothing. "But now watch as I slowly increase the speed of rotation."

As Doctor Wu turned the knob on the motor controller, the splash of light on the wall became brighter and no longer illuminated the full 360 degree circle around the room, but now covered just the width of the wall in front them, maybe five meters wide; then just four meters, and then two as the rotation speed was progressively increased.

When the image on the wall was only as wide as it was high, Wu made no further increase in the rotation speed. The image appeared sharp for just a few seconds before disappearing entirely. John Wu explained, "That was the last few seconds of a video that is five to six minutes long. It will repeat again in about two minutes and continue to repeat as long as I maintain this speed. As you observed, it only began to appear when the disc reached a specific rotation speed — about 225 rpm. When I further increased the speed, I found that the image began to spread out again."

Roger asked, "Does that particular speed of rotation have any special scientific significance?"

"No, not that we could determine." replied Doctor Wu. "Whatever sort of machine created this disc would use some other unit of time to count rotations — certainly not minutes. But watch closely, as the video is about to repeat. There is no audio."

What first appeared on the wall before them was an animation of a system of five planets orbiting a central "sun." The fifth planet was the largest and was surrounded by a flat ring. Beyond the fifth orbit was a belt of asteroids. An arrow appeared pointing at the second planet from the sun. Two small moons circled the planet, one very close and one more distant in an elongated elliptical orbit.

After a few seconds, the animation zoomed in on the second planet, progressively showing a closer view of the surface until a city, and then structures within it, began appear. The image faded out and was replaced with a flyover view of the city built along a river, with tall, spire-like buildings set in a mosaic of green space. This was not an animation, but appeared to be actual video. The next scene to appear was a classroom of eight or ten very young children seated on a long bench facing a female instructor clothed in a maroon robe. The instructor was writing symbols with a stylus on some sort of electronic whiteboard. The scene switched back to the children, waving at the camera before fading once again to black.

"The video will repeat again in a couple of minutes. The first time I saw it, I let it repeat for an hour. We've made a high-definition copy of it — just in case the disc stops working for some reason. You'll have a copy of the video to take with you today."

The visitors in the room were uniformly silent, contemplating the implication of the images they had just observed. Roger was the first to speak.

"I don't believe it would be an exaggeration to suggest that what you have discovered here, Doctor Wu, should validate the work of the Professors Chu and Tsum. Their work, together with yours, may well rank among the greatest scientific discoveries in history."

CHAPTER THIRTY-FOUR

Bayan Har Mountains, China
4 Years and 10 Months after the Arrival

IT HAD BEEN SEVERAL MONTHS since the mother ship received that first flash of reflected sunlight from the silvered mirror that Kandra had made using her knowledge of chemistry. The news that the crew of the third scout ship had not perished as had been believed for the first four years after the Arrival was celebrated by all members of the expedition. The crew members at Bayan Har received frequent and detailed reports concerning activities of their comrades at Giza and Tiwanaku, but very little information could be sent back to the mother ship from Bayan Har. The mirror signaling system was pretty much limited to answering yes-and-no questions transmitted by personnel aboard the mother ship.

Now that the earth expedition was in its fifth and final year, it was up to the discretion of the Commander of the mother ship to make the decision that their assigned mission had been completed and the Visitors could return to their home planet. The knowledge that their mission was nearly over was not lost on the scout ship crews in Egypt and Tiwanaku. In recent weeks, their periodic reports had been reduced to the mundane — much time had passed since their last new initiative or significant scientific discovery. And so after a private exchange with two of his scout ship commanders, the decision was made. In just one week, the scout ship at Giza was to proceed to Bayan Har to pick up the crew members there, then rendezvous with the orbiting mother ship. The ship at Tiwanaku would depart for the mother ship the next day. With all aboard, the fifteen year journey home could finally begin.

At Bayan Har, reaction to the news was mixed. Although only Landon was in a committed relationship with any of the locals — he and Jia-Li had been together for more than three years — many friendships had been forged between the Visitors and the country locals.

"ARE YOU GOING TO LEAVE ME and your daughter and return to your home planet?" Jia-Li cried when Landon told her the news of the impending departure of the Visitors at Bayan Har. Landon had come to the house that he and Hongmin had built for Jia-Li and his daughter, next to Hongmin's house.

Landon held his wife close and spoke to her softly, "Why would you think that I would leave you and Hui-Ying?"

"It is a fear I've held in my heart for many months, ever since you were able to make contact with your friends from your ship in the sky."

"I already spoke with my Commander and told him that it was my intention to stay. The Mission Commander aboard the mother ship will agree to anyone staying behind as long as there is one senior officer to return home. He showed me where it was written in the Mission Directive — the rules that all of us swore to obey when we were first selected for the mission. In fact, he was relieved when I told him. He was concerned that I wanted to take you and Hui-Ying home with me, and that would be strictly forbidden by the rules of the Mission Directive."

Jia-Li wiped her tears and laughed, "Why? Would you be embarrassed for me to be seen by the people from your home?"

"No, I don't know the reason; it was just in the rules. There were rules written for just about any possible eventuality."

THE RUMORS OF THE IMPENDING ARRIVAL of another Visitor scout ship and departure of all the Visitors soon spread throughout the local population. The rumors were accompanied by a great deal of misinformation. When the young village chief, Zhang Zhu, first heard of it and discussed it with his followers, he made dire predictions about the arrival and suggested that rumors of the Visitor's imminent departure were completely unfounded and not to be believed.

"If we do not attack and destroy the Visitors before the second ship arrives, they will be too powerful and we will never be rid of them. Let us attack and kill them all now so that when the second ship arrives, they will see how strong we are and leave in fear. And if they do not leave, we will destroy them also."

LANDON WAS AT THE HOUSE with Jia-Li when Hongmin brought the terrible news.

"I am sorry, Landon, but there was an attack on your people this morning at dawn." Hongmin was out of breath, having run all the way from the ship's encampment. "It was Zhang Zhu and his men. I was taking meat to your people and arrived after the fighting was over."

"Survivors?"

"None. I am sorry." Jia-Li began to cry. "When I arrived, there were many bodies on the ground, and Zhu's men were throwing things out of your ship. One of the men told me that all five of the Visitors had been killed and more than twenty of Zhu's men were dead."

Without speaking, Landon put on his jacket and the holster that held his side arm and started for the door.

Jia-Li pleaded with him, "Do not go. They will surely kill you as well."

Hongmin added, "There are too many of them. Can you not wait until your friends arrive tomorrow? Then you can deal with Zhang Zhu and his followers. They even have all the weapons from your ship. It would be foolish for you to go by yourself."

Landon stopped and turned around to face his friend. "I am not worried about the weapons. They are useless—they cannot be fired—unless in the hands of a crew member from the ship. I do not intend to engage anyone today unless I find myself close enough to Zhang Zhu to kill him. But I need to see for myself, from a distance. I will be careful."

Kai's ears were perked up at attention. He was watching his master's every move and followed close behind as Landon left the house.

CHAPTER THIRTY-FIVE

Bayan Har Mountains, China
the Next Day . . .

IT WAS 6,500 KILOMETERS from Giza to Bayan Har—a ten-hour flight for the relief scout ship that most likely would have departed sometime near midnight local time in Giza. Landon had waited most of the day for the expected arrival. From his concealed location in the woods he had a good view of the ship and encampment. It was the same place he had come the day before with his dog, Kai, just to see for himself what Hongmin had reported concerning the attack.

The last of Zhang Zhu's men left the area an hour before, taking with them the bodies of their comrades who had been killed in the engagement. Landon had to restrain himself as he watched the men drag the remains of the defenders—his murdered fellow crew members—arranging the bodies in a row on the ground near the entrance to the ransacked scout ship. Zhang Zhu wanted to send the message to the second contingent of Visitors that if they dared to stay in Bayan Har, they could expect the same fate to befall them.

Now that the attackers had left the area, Landon came forward for a closer look. His heart pounded and anger rose up again as he viewed the broken and bloodied bodies of his comrades. These were the closest friends he had, and now they were gone. Landon found some blankets among the articles scattered about and respectfully covered each body.

IT WAS MID-AFTERNOON when Landon first heard the whine of the scout ship engines. He stepped out into the large clearing about fifty meters from the encampment and waited. The ship made one circular pass overhead, and then slowly descended to earth. The craft came to rest, but with engines remaining at idle speed for a few minutes, allowing them to cool down. The Scout Ship Commander was the first to disembark.

"What's your name and what has happened here?" With the contents of the disabled scout ship strewn about, it looked like a crash scene.

"Landon, sir. I was—I mean—I am the COM Officer. A large contingent of hostile locals attacked our ship and encampment yesterday."

"Where are your Commander and the rest of the crew?"

"They are all dead, sir?"

"All seven? Dead?"

"Five are dead, killed yesterday. Two crew members—our Geology Specialist and his assistant — petitioned for discharge from duty three years ago and relocated permanently to a village 300 kilometers from here."

"Where are the victims? Show me."

The entire crew had joined the Commander, and Landon escorted the group to where the bodies had been left near the disabled ship. The Commander gestured for the bodies to be uncovered.

"The wounds are pretty horrific, Commander. I covered our people myself just a few hours ago."

"How did this happen, Landon? You people were here for nearly five years, and then *this* — just one day before our relief ship arrives?" The Commander was trying — with little success — to maintain his composure. "Where were you when the locals attacked?"

"I was with my wife and daughter — in a house outside the village — about a half-hour away."

"Wife, eh? You married a local woman?"

"Yes sir. One of the friendly locals brought me news of the attack yesterday morning, after it was over. We have long maintained good relations with the local population that lived outside the village, but the villagers themselves were under the control of a young chief who was jealous of our relationship with the other locals. Every attempt at rapprochement was rejected."

"If your people were armed, this shouldn't have happened."

"I saw the attackers cart off more than a dozen of their dead, so there was a fight." Landon paused for a moment before continuing, "It must have been a surprise attack. Our people were caught off guard and overrun. Your impending arrival was known to the locals, but no special security measures were taken. It was believed that Zhang Zhu, the village chief, would welcome the news that he would no longer have us Visitors—that is what they called us—to contend with."

"You may know that we too had a hostile local population to deal with. It's the reason why we relocated to the West—to a place called Egypt—where the people were much friendlier. Before we left the first location, there was an incident in which lives were lost. Fortunately for us, none of our people were seriously hurt, but many locals died with the unintended destruction of their city."

"Yes, sir. We all listened to a recording of your account of events that was relayed to us by the mother ship."

"You were the one who reconfigured some of your ship's electronics? To receive communications from the mother ship?"

"Yes, sir. We were able to receive transmissions, but not send any. It was the ships chemist. . ." Landon looked down at the body of his friend. "It was Kandra who came up with the scheme to signal the mother ship of our presence here."

"I need to contact the Mission Commander and report what went on here yesterday; our departure will be delayed." The relief ship commander redirected his attention toward Landon saying, "If you know of a place where our people can be securely interred, we can plan a burial service for tomorrow."

"Yes, I know of a place, but I have a question, Commander."

"What is it?"

"The people who did this — will they pay no price for the murder of our crew members?"

"What would *you* have us do, Landon?"

"I want nothing less than to find Zhang Zhu and kill him, along with his followers who participated in the attack."

"I'll bring up the matter when I speak with the Mission Commander. Until we have an approved course of action, I am ordering you to not respond on your own; no need to add another name to the casualty list."

THE BURIAL SERVICE FOR THE DECEASED crew members began late in the afternoon of the following day. The cave where the remains were to be interred had been prepared earlier that day by members of the crew of the relief ship. It featured a narrow passage that led to a round chamber in the side of the mountain. The chamber itself was not a natural one. It had recently been cut from the rock by miners prospecting for silver-bearing ore. The crew spent the morning smoothing the walls of the passageway and removing rock outcroppings until the chamber was roughly circular in shape.

The tribute text that Landon composed was inscribed on each of the five Tribute Discs using an engraving device designed for that purpose in the lab of the scout ship. The tradition of the Visitor's home planet called for a disc containing video and text chronicling the life—and prepared for the family—of each of the deceased. But it was decided that another set of discs should be left with the remains of their dead crew members that could serve as evidence of their visit to some future generation of humans who might find them.

Each of the five discs was encoded with a random selection of video imagery depicting life on the home planet and inscribed with Landon's tribute text. Technology experts aboard the mother ship estimated that it would take another two-thousand years—some fifty generations—before the primitive civilization they found on Earth was advanced to the point where the inscriptions could be decoded and the image playback mechanism might be understood. Landon thought it was an overly optimistic estimate.

The covered remains of the five Visitors were placed in individual shallow depressions in the floor of the round chamber—each with one of the five discs. Jia-Li and Hongmin stood next to Landon inside the chamber with the relief Scout Ship Commander while the crew members crowded in the passageway behind them. Li-Hua waited outside the cave with the two children. Landon held a torch as the Commander read first from the Sacred

Scrolls and then the text of the tribute that Landon had composed.

When the ceremony was over and all had left the cave, two crew members used their side arms to collapse the rock ceiling of the passageway and bring tons of rock and earth down in front of the chamber and mouth of the cave, sealing it.

"LISTEN CAREFULLY, HONGMIN." Landon had called his friend aside to speak with him privately after the burial ceremony. "Tomorrow morning after sunrise you must leave Bayan Har with your family and mine and travel to Chiang-Ri. Before the ship leaves this place tomorrow, the village will be destroyed. It will be unsafe for you to stay here. If any of Zhang Zhu's men survive the attack they will surely bring harm to you because of our friendship. Prepare tonight what you will need for the journey. You must also warn Ming Yu, the silversmith. Tell him to take his family and the wares from his shop in the village and go to my house. He will be safe there."

"Will we ever see you again, my friend?"

"I don't know."

CHAPTER THIRTY-SIX

Arlington, Virginia
Present Day

AMANDA LED THE TSUMS into the dining area of her Crystal City condominium. Roger, who had been seated at the table with his notebook PC, stood to greet the guests and shook the Professor's hand. For a minute they chatted about the view of the Potomac, clearly visible beyond the runways at the south end of Ronald Reagan Washington National Airport. Amanda beckoned for her guests to be seated and then disappeared into the kitchen, returning with cups and a pot of hot tea.

It was warm in the condo and Melanie removed the orange scarf from around her neck, folded and inserted it into one of the pockets on the outside of her leather purse.

"That is a beautiful necklace," remarked Amanda. "Or would you call it an amulet, because of the jade turtle?"

"In my culture, an amulet is intended to bring good fortune or ward off evil. So yes, it is an amulet. It belonged to my birth mother." Melanie looked over at her father before continuing, "I'm told that it is very old. As you can see, the gold is quite worn."

Professor Tsum was the first to bring up the subject that was the purpose of today's meeting. "Professor Atwood, has the demonstration yesterday at the facility of Doctor Wu eased your concerns about the authenticity of the Dropa Stone?"

"Yes, of course. The video is compelling." Roger restarted the notebook's Windows Media Player and turned his computer so that the screen was visible to Melanie and her father. "We've played it over and over again."

"Then you will proceed with the project?" Melanie asked, "To tell the true story of my father's work?"

Amanda replied, "Roger and I had already agreed that unless Doctor Wu had reason to question the authenticity of the disc, we would proceed with the project. In fact, we have already begun."

"Yes," added Roger, "and thanks to Doctor Wu, we can draw some interesting conclusions about the people in that video. If you look closely, you can see that the hands of the instructor and the children all have four digits, consistent with Professor Chu's account of the skeletal remains found in the Dropa cave."

Roger paused the player at the scene from the video where the instructor turned to face her students after writing two columns of symbols on the white board behind her. "Doctor Wu pointed out that the symbols appear to represent the counting numbers. You know—equivalent to one, two, three, four, and so on. As you can see, there are just eight symbols in each column."

"I'm not sure I understand, Professor," said Melanie.

"Consider this: Our number system is decimal-based—that is, based on the number *ten*—ten digits." Roger held up both hands with palms open and facing the others at the table. "But the children in this video are being taught a number system based on *eight*—an octal system. If you think about it, what could be more natural than a base-eight number system for a race of beings with a total of eight digits on their two hands?"

Melanie had been listening carefully to Roger's dissertation and unconsciously clasped her two gloved hands together. Roger continued, "It's been years, but I still remember a little of what I learned as a college freshman in a beginning computer course. The first computers were all octal-based because the simple binary on-and-off of electronic *bits* are easily strung together to make up octal computer *bytes*. What I am suggesting is that maybe having only eight digits on their two hands gave this race of people an advantage—speeding up the development of their science and civilization."

Professor Tsum remarked, "That is a very interesting speculation, Professor Atwood. I would agree that there may be some anthropological basis for it."

"Professor, there is something else that perhaps you can explain—something from Amanda's notes. You said that the village where Professor Chu lived during the war and met and married his wife was called *Chiang-Ri*."

"Yes, according to the oldest residents, *Chiang-Ri* was the name of that village, named from ancient times."

"We tried to find it on a map. It was a very detailed map that included many small villages in China and Tibet, but there was no village with that name."

Professor Tsum smiled, "You will not find a village with the name *Chiang-Ri* on any map. I believe it to be the same village that James Hilton visited while doing research for his novel, *Lost Horizon*. In that book, he writes about a village hidden in the mountains with a very similar name: not *Chiang-Ri* but *Shangri-La*. My daughter and I believe they are one in the same."

CHAPTER THIRTY-SEVEN

Home Planet of the Visitors
2550 BC

IT HAD BEEN THIRTY-FIVE YEARS since the thirty space travelers left their home planet to begin the Grand Expedition. Not all would be returning home, of course, and the list of those left behind was included in the first radio report sent home even before the mother ship left earth orbit. The radio transmission arrived at the home planet just one year ahead of the space travelers' ship.

A plethora of radio reports followed, chronicling the details of nearly every event of significance that had been previously reported only in summary form. The travelers had spent the first several weeks of the return journey compiling their reports as the IMP Drive accelerated the ship to top speed. Throughout the voyage home, a rotating staff of six ran all ship operations. The remaining crew members spent a month or more in their "twilight sleep chambers" at reduced body temperature until it was their time to be awakened to run ship operations. This staffing cycle was repeated throughout the voyage home. Nearly fifteen years would lapse on the home planet before their journey ended, but the extreme high speed of the return meant that only two years would pass for the travelers. The time-dilation effects represented a fortuitous consequence of theoretical physics, mercifully shortening the period of mind-numbing boredom that characterized travel in deep space.

THE ECONOMIC DISTRESS that had gripped the home planet for five years prior to the return of the space travelers showed signs of easing even before the Star Ship inserted itself into orbit about the home planet. The mood of the citizens seemed to improve steadily as the arrival day approached. They felt better about themselves, worked harder and spent more money. At least this was true for the older citizens of the planet—those who were alive when the Grand Expedition began. But the younger population had a markedly different attitude. When a news reporter asked a twenty-year-old student if he was excited about the return of the explorers, he replied simply, "So they are finally returning after thirty-five years. Now what?"

The Unification Government declared a week-long period of celebration dedicated to the heroes of the Grand Expedition. The opening ceremonies at the Capitol began with a moment of silence, acknowledging the sacrifice of the explorers who were killed at Bayan Har. The Senior Administrator then recounted the significant events of the expedition as dozens of never-before-seen images were displayed on the screen behind him and simultaneously flashed to every Enclave on the planet. The population marveled at the scenes of farmers tending crops in the irrigated highlands of Tiwanaku, crew members — their fellow citizen explorers — providing medical treatment to families at Bayan Har, and laborers using raw human power to move the stone blocks used to construct the Great Pyramid at Giza.

It was not until his concluding remarks that the Senior Administrator brought up the subject that was on the minds of the millions of Believers across the planet. "I know that many of you have expressed disappointment over questions still left unanswered by the Grand Expedition, even after the investment of time and treasure and the very lives of our brave explorers. But the evidence of the Creator's existence is not to be found in scrolls and tablets or the artifacts brought home from the far reaches of space. It is necessary only to consider the images . . ." The Administrator turned to the screen behind him where many of the scenes shown earlier were redisplayed in quick succession. ". . . figures of beings from a distant place, made in the image of their Creator, just as we were made in the image of ours." The Administrator left it to the audience to draw their own conclusions.

EPILOGUE

HONGMIN AND HIS FAMILY, including his sister-in-law and niece, were living in the temporary quarters that had been provided for them while the carpenters finished the structure that would become their permanent dwelling.

All able-bodied inhabitants of Chiang-Ri were expected to contribute their labor for the benefit of the community, and the new arrivals were not exempted. After working in the fields for a half-day each morning, Hongmin joined the carpenters to help complete the work on his own house. Li-Hua was a classroom assistant in the school that had been organized by the Geology Specialist (her son, Sheng, was a student there). And Jia-Li spent a few hours each afternoon helping the women who tended the vegetable gardens while her daughter played with the other children nearby. But Jia-Li was having a very difficult time emotionally. It had been a month since she had last seen her husband, Landon. *"Where could he be?"* she would ask her sister. *"If he were alive and still somewhere on this planet, surely he would have come to us by now."*

In the evenings when she was unable to sleep, Jia-Li would often look up to the grouping of stars that Landon had pointed out on the night they first met. Crying softly, she wondered if her husband was out there somewhere—rushing faster and further from her, in the direction toward the *Beak of the Turtle* and his home planet—never again to hold her in his arms.

THEIR NEW HOME was larger than the house in Bayan Har. It had a proper kitchen, a separate bedroom for Sheng and two rooms for Jia-Li and her daughter. It was market day and the family of five left the house in the morning to join the other villagers, sampling the food and examining the wares offered by the vendors who were set up along the wide cobblestone street that ran near the lake's edge.

Jia-Li kept her daughter close for fear that she might get lost in the crowd of people. She picked out a neck scarf as a gift for her sister, but when she turned to show it to her daughter, little Hui-Ying was gone. Jia-Li panicked until she heard the little girl call to her from across the street a few seconds later.

"Mama, Mama. I'm over here—with Kai." The dog was excited, licking the little girl's face. Jia-Li rushed to join her daughter but stopped momentarily as she heard her brother-in-law shouting at her from down the street. She began to weep when she recognized the other man with Hongmin. As Landon rushed toward his wife and daughter, Jia-Li clutched the gold amulet about her neck, thankful for the good fortune that she believed it had brought her.

ABOUT THE AUTHOR

THOMAS SETTIMI graduated from the Institute of Technology at the University of Minnesota and earned a Master's Degree in Physics from the University of California at Riverside. For much of his early professional career he was engaged in technical writing and engineering for the Department of the Navy and defense-related firms. He later became the General Manager of a manufacturing firm in Huntington Beach, California.

Thomas lived near Lake Arrowhead, California, for much of his adult life. He currently resides in Brookings, Oregon, with his wife, Charlotte.

Other Novels by Thomas Settimi . . .

- CONVERGENCE
- ROSWELL 1947
- THE AVIARY
- BEYOND 2020